EPAPHRAS:
(E H - p u h - f r a s)

THE
INTERVIEW

MIKE MILLER

Epaphras (EH-puh-fras): The Interview
Trilogy Christian Publishers A Wholly Owned Subsidiary of Trinity Broadcasting Network
2442 Michelle Drive Tustin, CA 92780
Copyright © 2023 by Mike Miller
Scripture quotations marked NASB are taken from the New American Standard Bible® (NASB), Copyright © 1960, 1962, 1963, 1968, 1971, 1972, 1973, 1975, 1977, 1995 by The Lockman Foundation. Used by permission. www.Lockman.org. Scripture quotations marked NIV are taken from the Holy Bible, New International Version®, NIV®. Copyright © 1973, 1978, 1984, 2011 by Biblica, Inc.TM Used by permission of Zondervan. All rights reserved worldwide. www.zondervan.com. The "NIV" and "New International Version" are trademarks registered in the United States Patent and Trademark Office by Biblica, Inc.TM
No part of this book may be reproduced, stored in a retrieval system, or transmitted by any means without written permission from the author. All rights reserved. Printed in the USA.
Rights Department, 2442 Michelle Drive, Tustin, CA 92780.
Trilogy Christian Publishing/TBN and colophon are trademarks of Trinity Broadcasting Network.
Cover design by: Kelly Stewart
For information about special discounts for bulk purchases, please contact Trilogy Christian Publishing.
Trilogy Disclaimer: The views and content expressed in this book are those of the author and may not necessarily reflect the views and doctrine of Trilogy Christian Publishing or the Trinity Broadcasting Network.
Manufactured in the United States of America
10 9 8 7 6 5 4 3 2 1
Library of Congress Cataloging-in-Publication Data is available.
ISBN: 979-8-89041-031-3
E-ISBN: 979-8-89041-032-0

DEDICATION

To Kathie, my beloved bride. Your love and encouragement made this happen. This book, and those following, are as much a product of your input as they are mine. Thank you for being such an amazing partner!

And to Gerry R., thank you for organizing and leading the Be Free Men's Group. You da Man!

TABLE OF CONTENTS

Prologue.................................1
Chapter 1: The Door......................3
Chapter 2: The Poem.....................27
Chapter 3: The Lump.....................37
Chapter 4: The Irony....................59
Chapter 5: The Workmanship..............65
Chapter 6: The Note.....................73
Chapter 7: The Small Talk..............103
Chapter 8: The Question................119
Chapter 9: The Refuge..................125
Chapter 10: The Meditations............139
Chapter 11: The Assault................163
Chapter 12: The Interview..............173
Chapter 13: The Toast..................185
Chapter 14: The Coffee.................199
Chapter 15: The Gunshot................205
Chapter 16: The Profile................215
Chapter 17: The Garbage................227
Chapter 18: The Joke...................239
Chapter 19: The Riddle.................255

Epilogue...............................275
Appendix:..............................281
About the Author.......................283

PROLOGUE

The seeds of this story were sown in 2011 when I wrote a series of character sketches for a blog challenge. I described twenty-six different people because the challenge was to produce a post for each letter of the alphabet, working from *z* to *a*, one per day, through the month of May.

I began with Zoe. The reader of this book might rue the day, but there she is.

Not all of the original cast of players made it into this book. Some were given prominent roles; some are only introduced and lightly referenced. Others are waiting backstage and are sure to be featured in future works. Can't wait!

In fact, there is a chart at the end of this book that tells a little bit about each of the twenty-six characters featured in this story and/or another three stories in the Epaphras series! The chart gives a general idea of which characters are either major or minor players in the four novels.

Since the writing of *The Interview* actually began late in 2022, I have been excited and very interested to discover for myself exactly what these folks would do and say! How would they respond to life's varied challenges? Who would or would not listen to the word of God speaking to their heart? How will each of them respond to their circumstances? Or to their conscience?

These are some of the important questions we each must ask and answer of ourselves every day. Hopefully, this story, inasmuch as it tries to stay in the light of the Word, will help us all find the best path.

May the biblical message contained in these chapters be a blessing to all those who need to give, or receive, forgiveness.

CHAPTER 1

THE DOOR

"Wait. What?" Charles demanded, nonplused. "You were talking about *what?*"

"Well, not breasts explicitly," I answered, but it probably seemed that way to the two other couples within earshot of our table. "I was simply once again rehearsing my 'B' theory, which is really much more about God and the pinnacle of His creation, for Teddy's amusement, and my own too, I will admit," I said, chuckling.

Charles and I were alone, or so I thought at the time, and talking in the well-lit but rather stark and cold room somewhere in the depths of the building about the events of a long-ago evening. I was as comfortable as could be in my chair, but Charles was already shifting and trying to find a good position that did not cut off the circulation to his legs on a cold metal bench at a cold metal table.

Seeing the look on his face, I paused a moment

before going on. "But I see that you're confused, Charles. I better go back and tell it from the beginning."

"Yes, please do, Epaphras. And thank you," said Charles. "I would appreciate that. We can go back later to how you first met Teddy when you were kids and all that, but I got a feeling the details of that night at Drakes are important for my article."

"You are probably right about that," I said. "But bear with me. It's always a pleasure to talk about my Teddy, but, well, it's not easy. And fair warning, Charles; I remember more details about that evening than of any other time in my life. And I might just unload every one of them on you."

"Fair enough. I have the recorder going, so I won't miss a thing," Charles assured me.

"Well, it was our second anniversary, and we were about to have a rather rare, nice dinner at Drakes, you know, the steakhouse in Chase. We had ordered our entrees; steak and loaded baked potato for me and baked chicken with mashed potatoes for her. Does that matter?" "Guess not," I added after Charles shot me a "what do you think?" look. "Anyway, we were both dressed up. Especially for me, with an actual tie on. Teddy always dressed up her clothes, more than the other way around, so she looked absolutely stunning as usual, in my favorite navy-blue dress.

"Queenie was just starting to help her folks at the restaurant then, and she brought out our salads. At ten years old, she was steady enough to carry a light tray, and she served our salads slowly and carefully. The practicing "waitress" even remembered which dressing went to which of us. Queenie was shy but so enamored with Teddy's model-like beauty and authentic charm that she stayed by the table after serving us. Teddy took advantage of the chance to bless Queenie up and down. She praised her for her excellent work in serving us and asked about her mother's new wheelchair, the coming school year, her 'new job,' and even about the waitress uniform and cute barrettes she was wearing.

I don't know who was more excited by the fact that Queenie would be in Teddy's fifth-grade class when school started again in just a matter of weeks for they squealed identically with delight. I never saw a kid so eager to get through the summer and get back to school! I just sat back and watched them both, but I was especially admiring my Teddy for her loving-kindness.

"Even at that point in the evening, I was sure that

Queenie's life would be impacted by this interaction. Teddy was determined to make every moment of her life, every encounter, meaningful. The way she put it, her purpose in every encounter was for people to be encouraged and united in love.

"And Queenie got a good dose! She was rocking back and forth on her heels and bouncing the now empty tray lightly against her knees as she answered questions and reveled in the attention. And, honestly, I began to calculate how rich I'd be if I had a dollar for every time Queenie said, 'Guess what, Mrs. Mallas!' or 'Mrs. Mallas, guess what!' as ten-year-old girls are so prone to do.

"I thought about trying to break it up so we could eat at least half of our salads before the entrees came out but realized that their conversation was much more important than my eating. I had long ago come to admit that Teddy was not on the earth only for my sake.

"So, I relaxed and began to take a more careful review of my Teddy, especially appreciating her generous character and her forgiving spirit as I remembered the embarrassing events of the last few hours." Charles, I think, was about to cajole me to "get on with the story already," but this promise of my mysterious humiliation got his attention, and he looked at me expectantly with pen at the ready. "Embarrassing events? Tell me more!" he said without uttering a word.

"Monday is an odd day to go out for a fancy meal, but we wanted to go out on our actual anniversary, July twelfth. Naturally, I still had to go to work, and, naturally, I got hung up when the building inspector was late, and I had to wait for him. So, I arrived home that night even later than usual instead of early as planned! It was considerably later than our expected departure time for Drakes. Teddy had long since changed and looked ready to walk out the door, and onto the red carpet, for that matter, but she wasn't about to just sit and wait for me to get ready. She was emptying the dishwasher when I barged in from the garage in my grubby work clothes. I was frustrated with myself for being tardy, but she smiled graciously and gave me the sweetest kiss. One I'll always remember.

"Then I had to balance my principled determination to hurry and catch up to our schedule with my selfish interest in stopping to just hold her and look at her. With a pat, she sent me upstairs, where I tried to rush but ended up cutting myself shaving and only making things worse. After..."

"Wait," Charles interrupted. "Now you're giving me a detailed flashback of the whole evening instead of telling the story. Where's the 'big embarrassment'? It better be more than 'I was tardy'!" Charles interrupted.

"Yes, I am. Just try to keep up, will you?" I teased with a smile. "I think the context matters here, Chuck. Aren't you writers always saying stuff like that?"

"I guess we are. Go ahead then."

And then I added, "But no, I did not burn the house down or anything that dramatic, but I did make a fool of myself, as I think you will soon agree."

"Well, I hope so!" he said, which didn't really come out right. And then he effectively retracted the misstatement by pursing his lips and shaking his head. "Go on already!"

"So, after causing us to be late, I started trying to impose my guilt onto Teddy by claiming, nicely, that she had made the reservations too early. I remembered, as soon as she did not rebut that argument but only looked hurt, that it was me who chose the time. No, I did not admit that fact just then, and of course, neither did she point it out, but for a better reason than I had."

"Wait, what do you mean by that?" Charles interjected. "Your reason for hiding the truth is obvious. It was 'cause you're a selfish jerk! But what reason did she have to be so nice?"

"Exactly. The only reason she had to avoid pointing out that it was my fault, even if it meant that she would be letting my implication defame her, is that she loved me. That's Teddy in a nutshell, Chuck. Teddy would rather suffer for me than to see me suffer!

"Have you noticed, Chuck, that sometimes being treated nicely sets a guy off?" At first, he seemed inclined to object, but then I think something occurred to him, and he mumbled, "Yeah, I guess…" I looked at him, appreciating the admission but did not ask for any particulars. I just continued with my own. "Yeah, so right after that, I found myself rushing again, but not out of respect for our plan or for Teddy, but with the secret hope that I would suddenly be ready to go, and I would find her busy doing another chore or something so I could blame *her* for our being late! I was acting like such a jerk!

"Fortunately, however, that didn't work out either. When I was finally ready after having misbuttoned my shirt twice and then tying my tie first too long and then too short a few times before getting it right, she had long been flawlessly prepared, and I found that she had kept busy making a shopping list, writing and sending a lovely, Teddy-esque email to my mother, and even collecting the clothes I had been throwing on the floor."

"You really are a jerk!" Charles politely agreed with my self-assessment. "Well, was a jerk." he offered.

"Thanks," I mumbled and added a soft "were" under my breath just to establish the grammatical correctness of the assertion. "But I am glad I can say that I gave up on my evil plotting before I came down the stairs. Teddy stood there all ready and waiting with a big smile. So beautiful!

"I was amazed again that the most loveable and loving woman was also the most beautiful I had ever seen and that she married plain old me! She looked me over appreciatively and smiled, and that made me smile! Then, of course, she noticed that my socks didn't match! I had on one black and one blue. I ran back up the stairway, growling, and Teddy, true to form, let out a big laugh that, by its generous nature, broke all the tension in the house. It both convicted me of my sinful designs and let me know everything would be all right. I had to laugh at myself then and confess my sin to the Lord, and I was still smiling and had my attitude in check again when I came back down." At this point, Charles was smiling. Not sure if it was because he was delighting in my foibles or marveling at Teddy's generous spirit.

"Teddy remained kind-hearted and patient despite my foolishness. And yes, Charles, she forgave me. Before I even confessed." I saw a glint in the corner of Chuck's eye but wasn't sure if it was because my eyes or his had teared up a bit. "I think Teddy taught me something about forgiveness every day." Charles stared at me as he listened carefully and then, after asking me how to spell "forgiveness," made a note in his book. I spelled it out for him, sardonically, even though I figured he was pulling my leg.

"Anyway, by the time we were walking to the car, she took my arm and leaned in close and told me how handsome I was. Her generous laughter and soft answers convicted my heart, and in the car, I am so glad to say, I took a minute to confess all the stupid thoughts I had, and I apologized for being such a dope."

Charles took that all in without saying a word except, "You mean 'jerk.'" "Yes, that. But a much-loved jerk," I rectified. Charles nodded a grunt and made a few more notes. Then, with a look, prompted me to go on again.

"All of that recent history passed through my mind

as I sat in the restaurant and stared at Teddy, who was then laughing with Queenie delightfully, showering her with love. Her bright green eyes, whole-faced smile, and encouraging words spoke volumes. I took her all in with a mixture of pride and humility. I was so glad she was my wife, but I still found it so hard to believe. 'Thank You, Lord,' I prayed.

"When Queenie finally skipped away to the kitchen, her heart filled with Teddy treasure, I realized that I was staring again and got busted! I glanced upward and found that Teddy had caught me admiring her lovely...figure. She pretended to be upset, and knowing full well that I was prepared to give her a great answer, she challenged me, again, to explain the attraction."

"So, are we finally getting to the point where you were giving out with your so-called 'B' theory?" asked Charles, hopefully.

"Why yes we are, Charles, yes we are," I told him. "Do you think you are man enough to handle it? Not that I intend to elaborate on all of that here. Maybe that will be an interesting topic for another article sometime, right?"

"You think?" he asked, acquiescing and making a large note with exaggerated underlining on his pad!

"I sat through all the mushy stuff for what…?" he muttered to himself and used his pen to emphasize his frustration.

Charles was disappointed, but perhaps as part of his endeavor to become a professional journalist, he did not complain much more than that. He gave a little shrug, shook his head, and underlined his note one more time as I prepared to go on with a sympathetic smile. "Poor Charles," I thought sincerely.

"Well, what else happened?" he asked me.

"A lot of things were happening. Everything, that is, but our dinners coming out! Oscar and Hannah, folks from church, were sitting quietly and somberly not too far from us. They had their food already, even though they came in after we did, and it smelled great! That was bothersome! I didn't know him then, but Greg and the woman who is now one of his ex-wives were also at a table nearby, and they were already finishing their soup.

"My longtime acquaintance and coworker, Yeti, who used to be my boss and who you met here, was over in the corner making a lot of noise about something or other. Drake stomped over there a few times to quiet him down, without lasting effect. Updike was wheeling up and down, visiting guests as usual, but especially Yeti. She had some positive but transient impact on his unruly behavior. But finally, and I was surprised to see that she was even there, *Zoe* all of a sudden marched past us and made one trip to Ralphie and Yeti's table where she effectually shut him down good!"

"That, I believe!" Charles declared.

"I found out later that Zoe had been in the hall to the restrooms watching Queenie and Teddy getting on so well, and glowering! And I was not surprised to hear some time later that it was her interference that kept our food in the kitchen. When I called to make the reservation for that night, I had Drake check the staff schedule to see who was working when. He knew that Teddy and I preferred a time when Zoe was off, but there she was. Perhaps too many other diners had the same qualms about her service, or her presence, and Drake just could not appease every customer."

"I really want to hear about all that—especially about the famous Zoe—and I am curious about why she still has a job there, but what about the… conversation?" Charles would not give up easily.

"We'll see," I said, giving him a look.

"Teddy and I were seated across from the end of the

bar near the rear of the room and along the waitstaff traffic lane to the kitchen. I am sure that if they wanted to hear, half the staff, Greg, Oscar, and their company were all within earshot of our 'delightful' conversation," I said, trailing off thoughtfully.

Then I surrendered and started telling Charles more than I had planned to. I didn't know if it might be critical at some point or not, but truthfully, I just wanted to think and talk about Teddy.

"It started with Teddy 'whispering' as loudly as she could, trying to embarrass me but without looking like it! Remember, she had just caught me being impressed with her…dress."

"'So, what is the big deal anyway? They're just… breasts.' Teddy waved her hands in the air and demanded of me. 'Think about this,' she said while watching me reach for my water glass. 'If there are an equal number of men and women in the world,' as I took a big drink, 'then there are enough breasts for every person to have one!' she concluded, describing her little vignette with perfect timing so that I almost spewed a mouthful of water across the table but thankfully just caught it back in my glass! 'Checkmate!' she mouthed and folded her arms with her usual flair!

"We had had a version of this discussion dozens of times, but that was the first time Teddy offered that particular vision as a premise to her argument! I was gratified to know that she spent some time thinking about and preparing for this periodic debate, but what a riot she could be! And no, it was not the first time she played me into a corner and pronounced 'checkmate'! More on that later, I think," I assured Chuck.

I was laughing and shaking my head once again at the odd picture she had drawn for me when Charles interrupted. "Well?" he said. "Did she have a point, and how did you answer it?"

"Oh, of course she did, and she was just teasing me, so her pretend point that men have no reason to be attracted by a woman's bosom was easy to address, Charles. I let her point make my point. If everybody had one, or a set, there would indeed not be any particular interest at all in breasts, so yes, she was right about that. We all know and understand elbows, for example, so they are not a big deal between the sexes. They carry no mystery, no mystique. It's the differences between us, the things we do not share, that draw us over to the other side.

"But even more importantly, it's the whole of her

female person, not just her body or her shape, that intrigue a man. The whole body, balanced with itself in symmetry, is important, yes, but that needs to be balanced again with the spirit, with the whole of her character, with the mind, emotions, and will of the woman. When she is at peace with the healthiest form of her body she can manage, when she is improving her character, strengthening her mind, controlling her emotions instead of the other way around, aligning her will with our Creator God, then there is no one more powerful nor more attractive. If she knows she is made in the image of God. And acts accordingly. No one, good or bad, can stop such a woman because she has already finished the race," I explained. I paused long enough to recognize that my deep and profound proclamations only bounced off the block walls and fell on the back of Charles' head as he checked the battery on his recorder. He yawned, and I imagined that I felt how the fictional Ray Barone might have felt after sharing his "butter theory" with his brother, Robert, and receiving no accolades. I plowed forward, nonetheless, if only to rehearse my worldview for myself.

"The same principles apply to men as well, of course, but without the extra attribute of beauty that God came up with after creating Adam and which was applied to Eve. A man is more like a truck, seemingly built for practical purposes. He might be good-looking or even attractive; our God cannot help that since He decided to make us in His image, after all, but a man is never 'beautiful,'" I went on. "What we have in common is the goal of fulfilling our individual purpose before God." All that effort earned me a simple "Okay" from Charles. Quite literally, zero applause.

"Anyway, Charles, I went ahead and gave you the gist of my 'B' theory. Are you happy? It's probably not as "exciting" as you were hoping, is it?"

"Not at all," he answered glumly, "but it was interesting.

Chuck added, "What else you got?"

"Oh, brother," I said and went on. "There was more to the conversation, of course," I said thoughtfully, looking at the floor with my elbows propped on my knees. And then. "I guess I'll tell you a little more." Charles did not risk interrupting the pause that followed this allowance for fear of discouraging the kindness but simply waited for me to focus.

"Okay," I said but thought some more before going on. "Teddy always liked it when I mentioned my two favorite subjects. At which point, if I actually used that phrase, Teddy would look down and back and forth at her chest and say 'Oh?' and then laugh hilariously as I blushed and looked away like a shy schoolboy!"

Charles and I both laughed at her antics, vicariously enjoying the old joke from afar.

"The two favorite subjects, Charles, and Teddy was aware," I said, trying to regain my composure, "are God, the Creator of all good things, and Teddy, representing womankind so very well! If you think about it, Eve was the literal pinnacle of God's creative work on day six! Once He made her, He basically said, 'My work here is done,' and then took the next day off! Right?"

"I guess so," Charles agreed, in the tone of someone who did not want to admit that he didn't have a clue.

"I always relished every opportunity I could find to show Teddy that I loved her just for being her particular self, but also for her standing in God's order." Crickets. "Anyway, that's how I think," I added, in case he wanted to know. He didn't, and I went on.

"We were still waiting for our food, but Teddy and I had some fun as I went off on a few tangents, personalizing my theory for her and more quietly for privacy's sake," I said. "Teddy giggled shyly at all the right points and would pretend to be lost in arranging the remnants of her salad. She glanced up at me a few times, smiling happily and shaking her head slightly in mock disgust. This only made her lovely brown hair seem to wave at me, enhancing her charm and enticing me.

"I had been so hungry on the way home from work with an empty lunchbox, but being so entranced with her as I was, I did not even touch my salad. I was too busy waxing poetic about God's obsession with symbiosis, creating us with a sense of what is beautiful *and* providing beautiful things to behold. I told her, though, that even her outward loveliness paled in comparison to the deep beauty of her spirit and her character, her intelligence, and her good humor. How all of her amazing qualities led me to worship our Lord who, having created her in His image, must be such an awesome God!" Chuck seemed taken by the reality of our being made in God's image and what that means. "I never thought about it like that," he said. So, of course, before he could sign up to become my disciple, I went on to burst the bubble of admiration that might have been forming in his mind.

"In the meantime, yes, I admit, I was able to take several glances, one good look, and even a stare while Teddy poured herself some water from the carafe before I was busted again!

"'Well?' Teddy insisted, her eyes now locking onto mine and daring them to aim anywhere else.

"'Can I help it if your beautiful form compels me to behold it? No, in fact, I cannot!' Teddy knew this was true and, at first, just smiled in response. After two years of marriage, the woman was well used to being loved, wanted, admired, pursued, and, yes, looked at.

"Then she let go of my eyes and bent over her now empty salad bowl. She peered into it as if the small puddle of leftover dressing could tell her something as interesting as I had been saying. Maybe it did. At this angle, with only her lovely hair and the top of her face in view, I could tell she was still smiling sweetly, and I knew that she was sending me a message: 'Go ahead and look, dear husband. I am pleased to be your wife.'"

I guess I sat with my thoughts for too long at that point because Charles had to prompt me by clearing his throat and saying, "Then what?"

"I looked at her deeply," I said, "and fell silent.

And rejoiced. And praised God for the incredible myriad of ways He shows His love." And Charles let me have a minute.

"While we had been talking well above a whisper, about breasts, of course," and again I paused but this time to laugh aloud at myself, "and I was expounding on my unusual theory, the guy I later met at church, Greg, and his wife who were just across the aisle from us had not seemed to notice. But now, with the quiet falling on our table, I saw them both staring over at us. She seemed to see my wife with sympathy, understanding the pressure of what to her may have seemed to be only 'lines' or demands. He took the opposite stance, the vulgar one, and looked at me all googly-eyed and even winked! As if just 'getting something' was all that could matter to a man and suggesting that he and I shared some kind of brotherhood of self-centeredness. I was suddenly mad and then embarrassed to even be a man. 'Who wants to be part of *that* club?' I thought."

I could feel the same tense anger rising in me again as I retold the story to Charles, who looked at me warily as if he might sometimes think thoughts like Greg presumably had and was afraid that I might find out. I was not about to go there with Charles. I had already been guilty of judging Greg and almost of imposing a pugnacious sentence right then and there, so I ignored Chuck's unease and went on. Besides, people judge themselves. We all know when we're guilty, as I had fully known when I was getting dressed to go out and plotting to protect my pride. The issue is that we don't always accept even our own judgment. Because we try to pretend it's not also God's.

"Well, what happened next, Epps? You're wandering again," Charles pushed me.

I took a deep breath and went on. "Before I could begin to physically react to the sad state of affairs between Greg and what's-her-name, Teddy suddenly stood up and dropped her napkin in her salad bowl. She spoke definitively, 'Epaphras, I need you to elaborate on your theory at home. Right away,' and started walking toward the door. Even though this surprised me, my first inclination was just to sit and enjoy watching her go. She walked with the same perfect posture and mesmerizing confidence that had caught my attention that day in the hallway four years before."

"Wait. What? I don't know anything about that yet," Chuck interrupted.

"Oh yeah. I'll get to that later then," I promised.

"Anyway, I quickly realized that my 'first

inclination' was just plain stupid, and I jumped up, knocking the table with my legs so hard that both water glasses and the carafe tipped over. "I'm going to feel *that* later!" I remember thinking as I fumbled with my wallet and threw too much money in the puddle, which was quickly spreading across the white tablecloth and over the edge. Way too much money for just two salads and even too much for the two full entrees we had ordered but never did eat. I saw the 'winker' smile broadly and sneak me a thumbs-up, and then he and his wife watched Teddy go, along with everyone else in the place, of course. He was leering, and she was looking aghast as if a vital ally had foolishly surrendered to their mutual enemy.

"I was sure that neither one of them had any experience with cherishing or being cherished, for that matter. And considering how it seems they had both weaponized their sexuality to the point of their being mutually disarmed, they were not about to start getting any real cherishing that night either, I thought. You know, Chuck, I was so young and naive that I wanted to stop and give them both a lecture on the difference between happiness and joy, or on satisfaction versus bliss, or maybe on the right balance between giving and getting, right then and there! But I was much more eager to catch up with my Teddy and take her home!"

"Are all these 'great observations' really an important part of the story? I don't think so!" Charles snapped, all of a sudden starting to get antsy.

"Maybe not, or maybe they are, Charles," I pressed on, though quite surprised by the interruption, "but aren't you as amazed as I am that my memory up to this point is so very detailed? Thirteen years later, thirteen years to the day, mind you, I still remember every word Teddy and I exchanged, every person in the room, everything that happened, and even every thought and feeling I had, right up to the point where I caught the door as Teddy let it go, and she was being shot and falling back into my arms."

CHAPTER 2

THE POEM

Charles had long known the whole story and was not surprised to hear what happened outside the old front door at the steakhouse, but I think he was a bit stunned by the way I suddenly dropped that last bit in his lap. I didn't mean to do that to him, but after pausing and staring blankly at the wall behind me for more than a few moments, Charles suddenly dropped his head and burst into tears. I was struck by the depth of his compassion, and then I was suddenly overwhelmed and followed suit, crying both out of self-pity and with joy as varied memories of Teddy lined up and presented themselves before me.

I thought about the sweet lovemaking we both enjoyed so much, even early that final morning, and then I remembered the bizarre feeling I had with our warm blood comingling between us as Teddy lay dying against my suddenly paralyzed body in the doorway at Drakes. And then I thought about the dozens of times she had put on that coy smile and said our forever catchphrase, "checkmate," to me at just the perfect moment! I never saw it coming, and I was never surprised that Teddy played it so perfectly!

And then I missed her so much and was jealous of her at the same time. Yes, I was still alive, and she was the one who died from that bullet, but it felt like Teddy had won the game because she got to go to heaven. She was "absent from the body and present with the Lord." Me and my broken body were stuck in a wheelchair.

Thirteen years had passed since that night when Teddy was killed. Exactly. This weeks-long interview was scheduled to start on the same date as our wedding anniversary, July 12, which of course, is the same date as the shooting too. I didn't know if Charles planned for the interview to start on the same date on purpose or not, but it was okay with me if he had. Some feelings should be kept close and are meant to be felt.

Then, just as suddenly as his tears had begun, Charles' head popped up, and he looked around, seemingly embarrassed, and quickly wiped his eyes. He recovered so speedily and appeared to be so under control that no one would be able to tell he even had an emotion to call his own. I wondered if that was the way to be in here.

"Well then…" Charles dove right back in. "Where should we begin to unravel the story? A few minutes ago, you said that your memory of the whole evening is perfect and that… let me see here, you can 'still remember every word Teddy and I said, everybody in the room, all the things that happened, and even your ideas and memories,' Let's go for the deep background first."

Then he went dark again, for a moment, while he thought up a plan. "I think you've told me everything you want to say about the conversation. Tell me more about Teddy. How did you meet Teddy?"

"I love to talk about Teddy!" I blurted, amazed at how quickly his compassion had been traded for composure. "That's a great place to start!" And I had told this story so many times that I was able to launch right in.

"I first met Teddy when I was only twelve and she was eleven years old. We were both in a state chess tournament, each there from our own school. Before our match came up in the third round, I had already won two games and was feeling cocky. So, when I checked the pairing sheet for game three on the board and saw that I was to play someone named Teddy, who had a lower rating than mine, I felt good, and I walked down the long rows of tables feeling confident that I would take another win. I was a little confused when I didn't see a boy at the table I was assigned, but when I stepped up and saw her with a nametag that clearly said 'Teddy,' I, well, I forgot how the pieces moved! Not just because 'Teddy' was a girl, but because she was such a very pretty girl!

"She was all ready to play, but we had to wait a full six minutes for the official start time. I set up my clock and fussed with my white pieces, making sure they were all perfectly centered on the squares. That only took a minute, so I did it again, three or four times!

"Teddy didn't say a word but looked at me and smiled and waited as if she expected me to offer some small talk or have some manners or maybe even to act as a big boy might. I had nothing, which was unusual for me. Normally I would at least have something to say about my name, but she didn't seem to think anything of it, so I didn't even have that to talk about.

"When the signal came to begin, I moved my

king's pawn up one space and felt ill because I did not land it in the center of its new home. Teddy picked up her king pawn and caught my eye. Then she waved the pawn toward my chess clock and gave me a little smile as she placed her pawn, haphazardly, on King 4. I slammed the clock button and immediately turned red because I had forgotten to push it after my move! That never happened before; this was *not* my first game!"

"So, what does that even mean?" Charles asked, alarmed. "Does it blow up or something if you don't push the button?"

"No, of course not. It's just part of the routine for a competitive chess player, and I forgot. It was another layer of embarrassment for me."

"Oh boy," was all the sympathy I got from Charles.

"I was supposed to be a much better chess player if ratings mean anything, but she went on to beat me good in just eighteen moves!" Chuck might think I was making excuses, but I …made my excuses anyway. "I think that even at eleven, she had an undeniable promise of coming beauty that knocked me right off my game!"

"Whatever you have to tell yourself," Charles chided. "But I do believe it, actually," he said, realizing that he had inadvertently suggested she wasn't all that gorgeous. "She was indeed stunningly beautiful." And then he quickly asked, "So, did you two become friends after that? What happened next?"

"No, not at all. I was so stunned about losing that game and so tongue-tied anyway around a girl like her that I didn't even say a word. I walked away and moved on through the day, losing all the rest of my games for good measure, and yes, I always blamed her for those losses too! My rating plummeted after being beaten by kids I should have taken easily. Teddy's rating, it turned out, was only low because she was just starting out in the program. Hers leaped upward while mine sank miserably. Anyway, I was too discouraged and too mad, for no good reason, to follow her progress that day, but when I was moping out to my coach's car later on, I did see her climbing into a school bus with only the name of a bus company I never heard of on the side. And she was lugging one of the biggest trophies I ever saw! I tried to tell myself that it was a good thing I did not win that three-and-a-half footer because it would have been a long ride home with that thing crammed in the car with the six of us. Oh, the lies we tell ourselves!"

"I suppose," Charles said, "but don't worry. Your plan to avoid taking that trophy home coincided nicely with her plan to whoop you!"

I gave him no more than a wry smile while he enjoyed a laugh. Then I went on trying to answer his earlier question, instead of his logic.

"All I knew about her was her odd but amazingly cute nickname, Teddy, and I watched for that name at every state tournament after that day, all the way through high school, but I never saw her again. Teddy told me later that she found her big day of victory to be as boring as I found it to be calamitous. Not very comforting, but her continuing absence was good for my rating. Without her there to distract me, and to beat me, probably, I ended up doing well in chess."

"Um. No one cares about your chess career, Epps, no matter how glorious. But how did Teddy come back into your life?" Charles asked.

"Yeah, yeah. I know no one cares, and neither did I, once we met again and the main benefit of my being involved in chess at all had been achieved!"

Then I felt like I was about to tell a sacred story and that I needed to set it up correctly. I moved over by the wall and turned around to face Charles squarely.

"Remember that I said she had a 'promise of beauty' even at eleven? Well, it was the mature expression of that promise I suddenly recognized one day nine years later in a crowded college hallway, right during the first week of my senior year," I told Charles, getting excited.

"I was moping my way down a set of stairs in the student center, heading down onto the very noisy main floor. As I turned at the landing, I could see below me the whole wide hallway full of kids rushing and weaving past each other in both directions. Everyone was either excited or anxious as the term began, and it seemed they all had something to say, loudly, about it.

"I thought I could pick out all the freshmen as the ones pausing and looking around and reading signs and looking totally lost. Seeing them all in a panic like that made me feel so wise and mature! And cocky. I actually snickered a little, as only a senior can.

"Of course, I was noticing all the pretty girls, but I had no aspiration for meeting any of them. I was just too serious about my classes and a couple of Bible studies I was preparing to lead that semester. But then I saw two girls step out of the relatively quiet study lounge, merge into the crowd together, and head down the hall away from me. The blonde was very attractive, but when I took a closer look at the brown-haired girl, I was stunned by her beauty! And then I suddenly realized, after all those years had passed, that it was Teddy! I couldn't believe it, but I surely acted as if I did!

"I ran headlong down those steps, bumping people out of my way, and chased her down the hall, calling her name! 'Teddy! Teddy!' Of course, I remembered her name, or what I thought must be a nickname, but that girl did not even slow down. I started panicking! And doubting if it was her. And feeling stupid. Maybe she had stopped going by Teddy by that time! There was no reason to think she would even remember me, but I'd been kicking myself for years for being such a fool the last time we met, and I wasn't about to miss out again without even trying. Finally, I started yelling, 'Check! Check!' The other kids I was pushing through were looking at me funny and probably wondering what they should be checking, and then I tripped over some guy's leg, fell headlong, and just missed bowling Teddy over! I looked up from the floor and saw her stop abruptly, turn her head in my direction, and her beautiful lips say, 'Checkmate'! Apparently, she also had our last conversation entirely memorized!

"Chuck, I was never so glad to have that word directed at me! At that moment, I rejoiced that I had only blundered through that game of chess! Otherwise, a plain-looking guy like me would never have had a chance in that hallway with such a beautiful, confident woman, and I wouldn't have had the chance to use such an outrageously blundering pickup line!

"Then, Charles, while I got up and tried to catch my breath, she stood there smiling at me! Not laughing, just smiling, which didn't help me settle down at all! If she was embarrassed by all the commotion or upset or bothered in any way, she didn't show it. Her friend looked a little shocked, but she stood with Teddy to see how this all played out.

"And when I finally did regain some composure, Teddy hit me with a little "poem" her eleven-year-old self had written on the bus ride home after our short game. Even after my rude treatment when we were kids, and even after seeing my clumsy, obnoxious, and disheveled self in that hallway, she said to me: 'Epaphras, the boy I miss.'"

CHAPTER 3

THE LUMP

I looked at Charles and saw that he was not impressed, though he did scribble something down. "Anyway," I said and waited for his plea for me to continue. I looked again. Still no plea. He looked at me stoically, maybe waiting for me to leave. And perhaps even regretting his decision to write my story. Chuck was hard to read. Or perhaps I should just say that he was more discerning than discernable. "Guess you had to be there," I offered and paused. "It was a much cuter moment for me than you seem to understand," I added, hoping to be understood, and paused again, giving him one last chance to be encouraging. Then I pleaded, "And Teddy liked it too!" Everyone who ever met her wanted to be aligned with Teddy, but even that prospect failed to get Charles interested.

Instead, he yawned widely while nodding politely. I rolled my eyes and suggested we take a break, and

EPAPHRAS: THE INTERVIEW

he jumped at the chance to stand up and get some blood flowing to his legs. "Must be nice," I thought. While he was led out to use the restroom, I rolled around the room a bit, waking up my arms at least, and ended up across the room, staring blankly at the painted cinder blocks.

I figured I could understand his boredom. Charles was not the one who had been madly in love with Teddy. He didn't have the privilege of getting to know her, to hold her hand, and to hear her thoughts whispered in the dark. He never knew, and never would know, the things she struggled with and had overcome. Teddy's life had come to be freely poured only into mine, just as those too few recent years of mine were poured into her all too short of a life. I went on thinking about how special our relationship was and asked myself if Charles could ever understand.

"Part of the wonderful charm of marriage is held in its very private nature," I pondered and rehearsed a few thoughts for a future men's group lesson I might give on marriage. "No one outside the very couple can ever 'get' what's being experienced within. It's true of the challenges and problems, yes, but more importantly, the inside jokes and the laughter can never be fully appreciated by anyone else even if repeated or described perfectly. The simple touches or the looks exchanged are not necessarily secret, but the communication is entirely private and personal. Being single, Charles couldn't even empathize, let alone understand, how significant Teddy's little poem was to me. Even now. But he started this project hoping to understand and describe how Teddy's death, and my paraplegia, had ultimately played out for the good in so many lives."

As I was thinking about my grandiose philosophy on marriage, I remembered part of a simple conversation Teddy and I had enjoyed together one Saturday in the weeks before Teddy died.

"Do you want pickles with that?" Teddy said, standing at the open fridge.

"Oh yeah, good idea!" I said, setting out some plates and reaching for her favorite bread.

We had been out shopping that morning, gone for a long walk praying for our neighbors, and cleaned the house together.

"Here they are," she went on, "and I know you want yellow mustard to 'mingle' with the dill pickle juice in your sandwich," handing over the second bottle and laughing at my culinary principles.

EPAPHRAS: THE INTERVIEW

"Oh, baby, I love how you know me and care about what I care about!"

The lunchtime sun came in steeply through the little breakfast nook window overlooking the backyard. Half the table was shadowed and dark in contrast to the other, glaring side, so full of light and warmth. I would be outside soon to mow the grass, and the light reminded me that I needed to find my shades.

"Of course, darling, but since we are one flesh, loving you is like loving myself, so why wouldn't I give you the best?" my girl said with a wink of one of her shining green eyes.

"Oh, I see how it is!" I played along, badly feigning hurt through a big smile and reaching out with a close hug. "You love me bunches, but only for your own benefit," I said with my forehead touching hers.

"That's right," she confessed and turned back to the fridge. "Did you eat all my cheese again? I would have gotten more this morning. Oh, here it is. By the way, I saw your sunglasses on the floor by the front door and put them on the—" as I spun her back into my arms and kissed her.

Conversation gold.

"We really were becoming one," I thought, and

then when I turned back around from the wall, I was startled to see that Charles was somehow back at his table by the door! I hadn't heard any footsteps or keys fumbling or even the door sweep scraping across the floor as he came in!

Charles looked all refreshed. His face was flush and damp, and his shirt collar, wet. My face felt all damp too, but salty, and I realized that I had been tearing up. Chuck said nothing about it and seemed like he hadn't heard any of what I had just been saying, but I couldn't be sure. I wasn't even sure if I had been only praying inwardly or actually speaking my thoughts to God out loud.

When he sat down, now sitting up much straighter than before, he wrote something down before quickly looking over his notes and saying, "Oh yeah. 'Epaphras, the boy I miss.' Teddy was a poet, and you didn't know it. Is that the best she could do?"

"Ha. Ha," I said and gave him another eye roll and a smile as I pushed over. "She was eleven when she wrote that! Besides, Teddy was too busy caring about people and giving to people and meeting their emotional needs to bother with being very creative with words." Then it was my turn to be embarrassed at inadvertently disparaging Charles and his ambition to be a writer. Thankfully, he didn't show any alarm, so I let it go.

"I don't know everything you know or don't know, Chuck, so maybe I should just ramble on from here, and you let me know if you want me to move on or stop and dwell on something. Sound good?"

"Fair enough," he answered. "And maybe skip any more poetry?

"Fair enough, yourself," I replied. "What about her outfits? Do you want to hear about what she wore every day? Cause she was quite—"

"No!" he pleaded. But then chuckled and amended himself. "No, thank you, I mean. Maybe just recap what came next with you two, and then we'll get back to Drakes. I only have so much time left today, and I'd like to hear more about Yeti and the others. I know a little something about them all already, but I only have a few rumors about their roots."

"Okay, Chuck. That sounds good. All their stories are remarkable, mainly because all people are remarkable, and I will be happy to share everything I know about the changes that came to be as they encountered God. I have gotten permission from just about everybody you asked about. Nothing from Greg, though. And I didn't even bother asking Zoe."

Now Chuck was getting ready to listen intently. He checked the battery on his recorder, shuffled his notes, and sat poised with pen in hand, looking so attentive and serious that I had to give him some grief.

"So, right after Teddy gave me her little tidbit of a poem in that hallway, I took her in my arms, kissed her mightily, and said, 'Checkmate yourself, baby!'" Chuck dropped his pen and gave me a stern look! "Okay, so that part was just in my head," I said, laughing freely at my own joke!

Charles gave me a resigned thumbs-up and a slight head shake and picked up his pen. "Oh really? You had me convinced! Wanna try again?"

"Well, the actual conversation is just a blur, but we did talk for a few minutes there between classes and made plans to meet that evening. I asked if she could give me some chess pointers, and she said I could sure use a few! But we hit it off at once! It was really like we were truly meant for each other, and the rest is history!" I said, reducing the best time of my life into two sentences and waiting for him to beg for more details.

"Well, that sounds rather normal, then. And boring," he threw in.

I didn't think so, but…to each his own, I guess.

"May be, I guess," I admitted, and my excitement was utterly stifled. I paused and then went on slowly. "But after that 'chance' encounter," I said, throwing up the required quotation marks, "Teddy and I began seeing each other right away—dating, I guess—and quickly fell in love. It wasn't long, only about four months, before we were engaged during that Christmas break and started making wedding plans. I was going to graduate in the spring of '96, a year ahead of Teddy, but decided to add teaching credentials to my plan, and we graduated from college together the next year.

"What a year that last year was! I lived off campus, and Teddy ended up sharing a dorm room with my sister, Macy! I had to take a heavy load of classes to get it all in so quickly…" Charles looked at his watch and then at the clock on the wall.

I pushed on. Talking faster. "We were both student teaching too, and Teddy worked part-time at the dining hall. And we were both involved in campus ministry too. We worked together to lead a Bible study and stuff, and we began to spend a lot of time talking, together, with all kinds of people, about our faith. That was so fun and so bonding for us both! And, on top of all that, we were planning our wedding for July of '97, which was pretty much right away after we finished school. And amazingly, God blessed our job search, and we both found teaching jobs in the same elementary school in my hometown, Chase!"

"Blah, blah, blah," Charles threw in. "Tell me about Yeti! Or maybe Zoe!"

"Oh." I was surprised. "Okay. Whatever you say, boss." I had told him that I liked to talk about Teddy, but I guess he had heard enough for now.

"Zoe or Yeti? Okay," I muttered, gathering my thoughts as I changed gears. "Zoe hasn't changed a bit, as far as I know," I told Chuck. "So, if you know her today, you know who she was thirteen years ago. But Yeti! He's a new man altogether!"

"I did know who Zoe was back in the day, but she's way older than me," Chuck said, "and it's been a while, as you might guess. She doesn't visit, I'll say that much. So, tell me about the 'big changes' in Yeti. Did he change denominations or something?"

"Ha! You have no idea!" I was excited to tell Chuck something he didn't know and about the one person in the story he actually met recently. "His nickname alone should give your readers a good idea of what Yeti looks like, which is really about the only thing that has not changed over the years! Yes, he is big and hairy. The look is a little out of place now that he's moved up in the world, but I'll let *you* tell him that!" I chided Chuck.

"Oh? I thought he still worked in the field, but maybe I was going by appearances too. What does he do now?" Chuck asked.

"He's still in construction," I explained, "so he can get by with the jeans and all, but he is a project manager for one of the big outfits. They like his work, so they don't bother him about the hair and the suspenders. Besides, all of the crews he supervises now love him just the way he is! It doesn't hurt, of course, that whenever he shows up at a jobsite these days, he brings bags of donuts or hamburgers and something to drink for everybody! Yes, he's a new man, all right! And that's the man you met when we first came here.

"His dad was the contractor I worked for summers when I was in college, and Yeti was my first crew chief. I worked with him building homes for three summers. Then for three summers after that, Wade, his dad, gave me my own jobs and a crew to lead.

"I remember when I first met him, though." I continued. "I was really intimidated by him, if only because of his size and appearance, because that was before I found out he had such a hot temper. If Yeti was in my way, I would just go around, as you would drive around a dump truck stopped in the middle of the road, slowly and carefully and kind of peeking up at the driver for permission to enter his right-of-way."

Chuck was excited, too, now that we were getting into the nitty-gritty. Even with the recorder going he was furiously taking notes and kept prompting me to talk even faster. He would never let me see his notes, but they must have been something for all the scribbling he was doing over there! I think he wanted to have many hours' worth of work to do to get him through the long evenings alone.

I went on. "Yeti was a good carpenter, but a terrible foreman! Of course, he gave me a lot of grief over my name, and my coworker Isaac too, but that was predictable, and we were both used to that. Worse than anything like that, though, was his concept of being a boss, which in his mind was far removed from being a leader, let alone a servant/leader." I realized that Chuck was unfamiliar with this idea, too, judging by the blank look on his face, but proceeded anyway.

"He would get Isaac and me going on something and then change his mind and yell at us for doing the wrong thing first. He hated answering questions, so I hated to ask him anything, but I had to all the time. I forced myself to even if I knew it would set him off on a tirade. Neither Isaac nor I would simply 'look busy' or stall, or hide, or go ahead and do the wrong thing with the excuse that 'Yeti *said* to do it that way.' So, for one reason or another, he was always mad. Especially if we had to point out a mistake he made! Oh, boy, that was always something!

"I know he wanted to get rid of me more than once, but I never gave him any real justification that he could present to his dad. Plus, his dad knew what we were putting up with and started giving me and Isaac raises to keep us coming back every day, let alone every summer."

"I doubt if you know anything about Lenny, do you, Charles? Didn't think so. I'll tell you all about Lenny sometime, but I mention him now because without my experience working with him on the farm back in high school days, I would never have been able to endure working with Yeti through my college summers." Charles nodded slowly and made a note to himself.

"Eventually, I realized that Yeti had more bark than bite. He never did hurt anybody, which was surprising considering all the dreadful threats he tossed around. And whatever fears I may have clung to that first summer vanished the first time I saw Yeti in the pool! That great mass of hair, which was always just piled up thick and long like a '70s rock star wannabe, melted like the wicked witch when it was all wet, and it laid down tight to his scalp. I didn't let him catch me staring, but I saw that the top of his head was shaped like the ridge of a house roof! He had this sharp row like an 8/12 pitch ridge line running right down the middle of his skull!

I wanted to laugh out loud, but we weren't the good friends then that we later became. And you know that great big smile? Well, he never smiled back then either, and I knew that laughing in his face would not be a good idea. I might have been the first person he did hurt! But I'll tell you, Chuck, if I saw that wet head again now, I'd laugh my own head right off!"

I was in my element now, thinking about all the changes I've seen come to pass in the lives of people like Yeti. I couldn't pace, exactly, in my chair, but I could sure push myself back and forth and around the other tables in the room as I talked.

"In those days, Yeti was always frustrated with

the day's work, or with his dad, or with his 'lazy loafers,' as he called Isaac and me. More than once, he let the delivery guy from the lumberyard have it, like when a load of two-by-fours was slid carefully and deliberately off the back of the angled truck bed but splashed mud into Yeti's lunch box, which was sitting open just off the driveway. For all the shouting and threats made that day, you would have thought that one of us had been crushed under the pile of lumber instead of his Twinkies getting a little spattered with mud."

Chuck tried to picture the current Yeti screaming and fuming like that and thought it was hilarious, as if there was some kind of a joke being played. Not me. While always rejoicing with Yeti over the changes God brought into his life, I could still feel the familiar ominous vibe when I just talked about the old Yeti. I tried to describe the internal tension Isaac and I both felt all day, every day, under the threat of Yeti's freedom to be an absolute skunk all day. "It was like walking on eggshells, except with eggs that were filled with either hot lava or baby velociraptors. We knew we were bound to get burned or bitten or both!" I explained.

"The upside is that Isaac and I both learned fast and became good carpenters if only to avoid facing any warranted wrath! It sounds funny, I know, but it's much better to be unfairly berated than to deserve it."

Chuck again looked at me quizzically but did not say anything.

"Isaac could deal with Yeti just by being good. If he did actually make a mistake and deserved the blowout, then he would apologize and try again, ignoring the excessive outrage. If he was innocent, then he would forgive Yeti and move on. Simple. It wasn't so easy for me. I had to analyze everything to death and always wondered what caused his outrageous behavior.

"Until, that is, the day Yeti laid out a long thirty-foot wall all wrong, and we built it under Yeti's direction, mind you. We were nailing the last of the exterior sheeting onto the framed wall as it lay on the second story floor, and I realized all the doors and all the windows and all of the nailers where interior walls should be attached, all of them, were in the wrong places. I didn't say anything right away but snuck over and double-checked the plans when Yeti was in the porta-potty. Sure enough, he had laid the whole thing out backward!

"I don't know how many times Yeti had told us,

'You ain't here to think, so *don't!*' But I just could not stand by when we were about to stand up that whole wall. I had to figure out a way to let him think he discovered the problem himself. I had noticed that with the wall framed in backward, a sliding door that should have faced the new deck was now lined up with what should have been the solid back wall of a walk-in closet. So when Yeti was back, I said to Isaac, 'Hey, did you ever see a master closet with a slider opening on the outside wall like that? The architect must be a big *Green Acres* fan, eh? I guess some people just have too much money!'

"Isaac played along nicely, saying, 'I didn't even know there was going to be another deck on this end of the house.'

"Yeti started to tell us to shut up and keep busy, but the seed was planted, and he started looking around. While he ran back and forth between the plans and the new wall a few times, I signaled Isaac to slow down and just 'sound' busy for a bit. After all, every nail we put in now, we would have to pull in a minute.

"Yeti's new-found self-control and patience with mistakes were amazing at first. After he suddenly 'discovered' a problem with the wall, he just came over to calmly tell us to start pulling nails. 'There's no such thing as an exterior sliding door in the back of a closet, stupid,' was about all he gave us. 'It's in backward.' The fact that he didn't even try to blame one of us betrayed an admission of guilt. Plus, he went and got a wrecking bar and dug an old catspaw out of the bottom of his toolbox, and joined us in the demo party! We were only at it for about twenty minutes before the roof caved in on poor Yeti."

"Uh-oh," Chuck intoned, guessing what was coming.

"His dad and boss, Wade, the owner of the construction business who employed us all, happened to come out to the job that day of all days and saw that we were tearing the wall apart, as opposed to building a wall. That day, I saw that Yeti had probably never seen a fatherly example of self-control or discretion in his life, and from where he gained permission to heap abuse on anyone he thought deserving."

"Uh-oh!" Chuck said again, with an empathy that reminded me of the special discerning powers I had observed in him, and yielded to, the day we met.

"None of us heard his truck pull up, but all of a sudden, when I stood up to stretch my poor back, I saw Wade's head and shoulders above the deck where he was standing on the ladder, leaned up in the soon-to-be stairway. He was watching us pulling nails and ripping sheets of plywood to shreds in an effort to remove them from the wall. Yeti's patience had just petered out, and he had begun to yell and cuss at Isaac and me. He was hoping the wall might be fixed before anyone important heard about it. Too late.

"Wade heard and saw all of it. He didn't ask what was going on but quickly figured it out and launched into his own obscenity-laced tirade aimed straight at Yeti! I thought about intervening with a soft remark about how 'mistakes happen' but thought better of it. Yeti took it for a few minutes and then bent over and started hammering on his bar, pulling nails, separating studs, prying headers off of plates, and otherwise tearing wood into splinters to cover the noise of the lecture he was enduring.

"But Yeti could not take it like he could dish it out. Eventually, he broke and started yelling back at his dad! 'Bad idea,' I thought. Then Wade, the real boss, told Isaac and me to clear out for the day and told Yeti to fix the whole thing by himself. 'Before you go home, and off the clock!' he added, 'So I can at least pay those guys the full day's pay they expected for today!'

"Isaac and I scrambled out of there quickly, and looking back, I saw Wade get in his truck, slam the door, and screech out of there while Yeti stood screaming at the sky!

"Wait. Yeti?" Charles asked incredulously. "Yeti was like all of that?" Chuck interrupted.

"Yes, he was. And proud of it too." I tried to emphasize that part because that is the crux. "People turn out all kinds of ways, Chuck, but it always depends on how they choose to respond to their circumstances. Think about this: Some people smoke because their parents smoked. Other people never smoke because their parents smoked. It's how we choose to respond to life that counts. None of us can blame our sin on someone else. Some look inside and are ashamed of their faults, and so they repent, but others see the same habits growing and manifesting in their lives and are proud of themselves and somehow justify it all."

This was about as close to preaching as I meant to get with Chuck. I couldn't tell if he even heard me, but he took us back to the subject of Yeti.

"Are we really talking about the same guy I met when the two of you first started coming around here? When we first saw you guys together, we called you 'David and Goliath' 'cause he was so big and you were so…"

He trailed off, so I filled in for him, "…youthful?"

"I was going to say 'little,' but I could just say 'low' because of being in the chair and all. Anyway," he continued, "after some of us talked with Yeti, we felt how much he cared about us, and we ended up calling him the Gentle Giant!"

"Yes," I agreed. "That's the new Yeti, all right."

"Hmmm," Charles intoned. "Interesting."

While Charles was taking that in, I thought of some trivia about Yeti, which did actually come into the story that night at Drakes, and I shared it with Chuck. "There were two things that actually scared Yeti. One was the possibility of losing his wife, Ralphie. The other thing that scared him, and I never knew, even after working with him building homes all those summers, I found out that night on the sidewalk. He can't stand the sight of blood!

"Everyone at Drakes heard the gunshot, but Yeti was the first one outside even though he was farthest from the door. Maybe he thought he would be able to grab someone and tear them to pieces, or at least scream in someone's face, or in some way be able to relieve the tension imposed upon him by the fancy restaurant scene, but as soon as he stepped over Teddy and me piled in the doorway, and saw the blood running out from underneath, he passed out cold!

"I was not conscious very long at all, but I vaguely remember being aware of Yeti stepping over me, hearing a kind of choke, and then seeing him stumble and fall hard close by. Then I had a glimpse of Ralphie leaning over a big lump on the sidewalk."

CHAPTER 4

THE IRONY

"As you know, Charles, only one shot was fired that night, but most efficiently. The bullet went right through Teddy, hit me, and lodged in my spine." Not sure why I felt the need to recount this basic fact, but I did. "Teddy only lived long enough to speak one syllable. She said 'Ep.' Some friends have suggested she was saying my most commonly used nickname. But I don't think so. She is the one person in the world who has always, and I mean always, called me by my full name. She wasn't about to give that up on purpose." I knew I was wandering off on a tangent at this point, but Chuck did not intrude. "I think she was calling out to 'Epaphras, the boy she would miss,' but couldn't finish it." Charles waited and let me dream a little.

Growing up with the name Epaphras was terrible. Kids are often so mean to each other. For no good reason, they can just turn it on. I learned to expect trouble, or at least face a meddlesome chore, every time my name was put out there. I could usually win kids over by laughing at my name with them, and then they would settle down and call me Epps or Eppi or Phrasier or any one of a dozen acceptable derivations. Eventually, I began to direct people to the books of Colossians or Philemon, where the name is found, and if that didn't win me a friend, it would at least get them to shut up for a while. So, I endured, and thankfully, because of Teddy, the burden eventually turned into a blessing, and I ended up being very glad for my weird name.

I thought I'd explain the significance to Charles. "I never really did stop feeling disturbed about my name until that precious day I ran into Teddy in the hall, and she said her line as if she had said it to herself every day for nine years: 'Epaphras, the boy I miss.' All of a sudden, I began to love my name!

"Because Teddy never called me anything but Epaphras, it began to spread. In fact, when my parents heard the way it sounded when Teddy said it, even they dropped the nicknames they had used. Then I began to introduce myself with a 'Hi, I'm Epaphras,' without any hint of embarrassment, and without looking at the floor and waiting for any one of a dozen, usually callous, exclamations. I learned to look the new person in the eye and follow through with a respectful 'What's your name?' as I had seen Teddy do. Her given name was no walk in the park either, you know. With such a simple thing, Teddy began to change my life immediately!"

"Really?" Chuck said and then asked, "What's her real name? I never heard about it!"

"Oh really?" I was surprised to hear that and thought I would make a game of answering the question. "Could you guess if I told you that while the nickname 'Teddy' came about for different reasons, it isn't far off her real name?" I didn't really expect Chuck to try to guess, but he dove right in, and I was surprised at how many "T" names he came up with in a minute.

"Let's see. Terese, Tegan, Tess, Tallulah? No. How about Theodora? Maybe Tedapaphras. No. Tianna? Tiffany, Biffany, Betty, Sally, Sue? Oh, I don't know!" he said, quitting as quickly as he had begun.

I laughed out loud. "Very good try! And you came close before you ran off the trail at the end there."

"Yeah? Which one?"

"I guess Theodora was the closest," I told him. "Her folks started calling her Teddy when they found her using one of her mom's nightgowns as

EPAPHRAS: THE INTERVIEW

a play dress when she was a little girl. And it was pretty close to her real name of…Theda.

"It's Greek and means 'supreme gift' or 'give to God.'"

"That's very pretty," Chuck said, kindly.

"Yes, it is," I said, and continued. "Both meanings came to have deep meaning for me. Firstly, because she was God's best gift to me! And secondly, because the day came when I had to give her back to God." My eyes suddenly filled up again, and I turned red as I tried to choke back the emotions. "Dang! I thought I was past all this," I thought. "But faith only makes things possible, not easy," I remembered as I shook it off and wiped my eyes. Charles remained professional now. He told me it would be okay and all, and then he started packing up his stuff and looking at the clock and stretching and talking about tomorrow's plan.

"We are scheduled in this room for 1 p.m. again. I think you said you could come at whatever time I could work it out, right Epps? I mean, Epaphras." That just didn't sound right coming from him, but he smiled apologetically, and we both laughed as I wiped my eyes again and then dried the back of my hand on my pants.

"Epps is fine, Chuck," I said.

"Okay," he said. And then he got me with, "And so is Chuck, by the way!"

And then, perhaps thinking he would lighten the mood even more as we were about to say goodbye, Chuck asked me, "So what does Epaphras mean, anyway?"

"Oh, Charles, I don't think you want to go there. The irony is too much."

But naturally, he wouldn't let that pass by! "What do you mean?" he asked quite seriously.

I had to answer from my wheelchair. "It might be said to mean 'stand.'" That caught him off guard a little, and he stifled a laugh, and then I finished with, "On foam," and we were both laughing hysterically as the confused-looking guard opened the door and led Charles back to his cell.

CHAPTER 5

THE WORKMANSHIP

I pushed myself as far as I could down the hall, looking for the way out, while two prison guards walked quietly behind me. I could feel their unease. People always want to push for me but hesitate because they don't want to be patronizing. On the other hand, I always want to be independent but could sometimes use some help. Nobody knows what to say or how to say it, so we all live with this stupid tension. I'm the one who is always in the chair, so it's up to me to address the issue, but that day in the jail, I just pushed and pushed without even thinking about it. I had too much on my mind, and the whole prison thing was starting to get to me. Yes, I know I wasn't the first person there to ever want to say, "Just let me out of here!"

We went through a few more barricades, hatches, and other assorted portals before finally arriving at a cage where I signed for and received back my phone, wallet, pen, and a pack of cough drops I had brought in with me. Once I had my phone and they said I could use it, I called Barn to let him know I'd be outside soon so he could bring the car around.

Then we came to another series of secure gates and locked doors. One of the guards said, "Thanks… partner," and disappeared through a side door. Guard number two took control of my chair, without asking me at all, and pushed me through the last confusing dose of passageways to the outside world!

As we went through the final, heavy exterior door, with buzzers loudly clamoring, we came into the sunshine, and the guard broke his silence, saying, "I am praying for you, Mr. Standing in Foam!" I spun around as he stepped to the side of the chair, and I saw that it was my friend, Krispy!

"What the…? Kris! You got the job! I didn't even know! Congratulations, my friend!" I blurted out my surprise and joy through his bouts of hearty laughter. "Last time we talked, you weren't sure if they would hire such a reprobate!"

"Yeah," he said, recovering but still celebrating his big surprise. "I found out that they really want rejuvenated criminals to be guards. It's good evidence that the system works. But all kidding aside, sir, remember I am not a convicted felon. I was arrested twice back in the day, yes, but the charges were dropped both times. Thank God."

"Amen!" I agreed. "Well, I am so happy for you! And you look sharp in that uniform! Do you like it?"

"Thanks! It feels good. Only two weeks in yet, but so far, so good. Yeah, I think I do."

"So, did you overhear my conversation with the inmate, Charles? The 'foam' line? I didn't see you… Oh. That room is monitored from somewhere, isn't it?"

"No, I didn't hear the conversation directly, but yes, it is, and I already heard all the juicy highlights from the interview! Contraband is always an issue here, right? You know, shivs and shanks and other deadly things like that. But the number one contraband in prison, as far as I can tell after two short weeks, is gossip! Everyone here knows everything! The guards already know all about your name and everything else you guys talked about," Kris explained while I quickly reviewed the day's conversation, checking for "contraband" ideas.

"I guess they heard us both crying, too," I thought. "Oh, brother!"

"I heard, too, that the warden wasn't really in

EPAPHRAS: THE INTERVIEW

favor of this whole thing, right?" Kris asked. "You must have friends in high places. But as I said, I am praying for you two. Hey, I better get back inside before they think I'm over the wire!" Kris waved in the direction of the parking area. I looked over and could see Barnabas wave back as he stood leaning against the car. "Tell Barnabas I said hi," he said, and with only that much warning, and one of his classic crisp handshakes, the buzzers were sounding again, and the door clanged shut behind Krispy as he vanished out of sight.

As one friend left, I looked up and saw Barnabas hustling in my direction to help me out, no doubt. I pushed myself slowly in his direction, smiling brightly, and thought, "I have good friends everywhere I turn!" Then, as I praised God for His steadfast love, all the built-up pressure from the long afternoon was released in a torrent on poor Barny as we met up and he started pushing me.

"Hey, Barn, how was your wait? Krispy says hi. What time is it anyway? I am totally lost. And starving! Is your tapeworm hungry? Let's stop somewhere quick before we head back!" And then, knowing I shouldn't push his buttons but too tired to resist, I added, "Hey, how 'bout if *I* buy me dinner and *you* buy me dessert?"

After we ate—and yes, I bought Barnabas a Reuben and a slice of strawberry rhubarb pie—and we had settled in for the long ride back to town, I thought about how the interview was going so far.

Charles and I jumped around a lot and talked about so many different aspects of that day that I did not envy him the task of writing a coherent story from his notes. But as long as he and I are on the same page when it comes to the article's overriding theme, I am okay with all the rest. I wasn't going to worry about what the warden or the guards had heard or would be hearing from that room as long as they heard something about the love of God and how He works in the lives of men.

"It looked like you were surprised to see Krispy in uniform, Epps. Didn't you know he got the job?" Barnabas asked me, glancing sideways with a sly smile.

I had to admit: "I sure was surprised! And he pushed me halfway through security, too! But without saying a thing, the rat!"

"When I saw him coming out pushing your chair, he looked like he was gonna burst, trying to contain the surprise as long as possible! I never coulda held it in as long as he did, that's for sure! And then when he talked to you, and you recognized him, you almost jumped out of your seat, paralyzed or not!" Now Barn was laughing hysterically and just caught himself curving toward the oncoming traffic. That reminded me all of a sudden of the days when Oscar was my driver, and I gripped the seat unconsciously! "What did he say to you anyway? I was too far away to hear anything but laughter. Kris was gunnin' for you, Epps. I told him last night that I was driving you up here today, so he must have planned the whole thing out with the other guards, the rat," he offered, pretending to agree with my pretend assessment.

"What about you being a rat?" I asked, pointing. "You knew Kris had started here but didn't give me a heads-up all the way up here? What's that about?"

"And it wasn't easy for me, Epps, you know that!" he said, laughing. And then in an effort to defend himself, Barn threw himself under the bus! "I never could tell a joke or get a punchline right, or even keep a secret! I had to bite my lip all the way over here this morning!"

"Well, then I guess I'm proud of you, then, I guess," I said redundantly. "Good job conspiring against me," and I prodded his arm. "And I thought you were praying the whole way!"

"You do realize, though, that our MG

confidentiality rule does not apply to general news like jobs and things, right?" I said teasingly, pretending not to understand that they had worked together to set me up.

"Oh, I know that; I think. We were just, well, Kris thought it would be fun to—"

"I know, Barn," I said. "I'm just having fun with you now! Just a touch of revenge."

He looked a little confused but smiled at me and shook his head at himself. "I'm still a work in progress, Epps, you know that."

He was actually a fine example of God's workmanship! I sat and looked across at Barn, driving with confidence but always carefully and responsibly. "You're doing great!" I said as he started squinting at the dipping sun and trying to keep the visor suitably adjusted as the road rose and fell, winding through the landscape.

CHAPTER 6

THE NOTE

The next day, Friday afternoon at 1 p.m., I was delivered to the same room somewhere in the bowels of the state prison. Chuck was all business right away. "I have a few rather general questions for you, Epps, before we get back into it today. Is that okay?" Charles asked me once we were both settled into our places in the prison conference room. The "bugged" prison conference room, I reminded myself when we came in, and I started looking around for hidden microphones. And I wondered if Charles knew about the surveillance.

There weren't any lamp shades or picture frames or window curtain pulls that would serve to hide a tiny microphone like they use on TV, so I decided that the "hidden" microphone was probably built into the very visible and obvious camera I finally noticed hanging from the ceiling of the room opposite of where Charles was sitting. I'm brilliant that way. And I figured Charles was well aware.

It had been a long night, and I was still tired. Barnabas dropped me off at home after we stopped at three different drive-throughs for ice cream, first of all, then a chicken sandwich, and finally a couple of tacos. Maybe Barnabas really does have a very hungry tapeworm inside! Anyway, it was pretty late by the time I got into bed, and then I couldn't sleep.

I had so many volatile or delightful thoughts swirling around in my head as I lay there. I had been very happy to talk about Teddy so much that day, and Yeti too, and I knew I would soon be telling powerful stories of transformation and healing about guys like Victor and Ned and Arty, and about the women like Hannah and Updike and Ralphie.

Of course I would talk about the hard cases like Greg and Zoe too. I always wondered how people like those two lived without the Lord in their lives! And then I answered my own question, "Well, generally, they live badly." I was so glad to be firmly rooted and built up in Jesus! As far as the article goes, I did not have to worry about cherry-picking any story over another. Every story tells us something about how a relationship with the Lord, or the lack of one, impacts a life. It would all be good and should be beneficial to Charles himself as well. When I started thinking about that and listing my many blessings, I finally fell asleep.

"Whatever questions you care to ask, Charles. You're the boss," I said and then asked him, "Could you make any sense of your notes last night? I was worried about the haphazard nature of our conversation yesterday."

"I didn't even look at them last night. I only thought about it. So didn't get much sleep. This morning, I did outline a few things, though," and he looked at me across the room and glanced at the camera behind me. "Which led to this list of questions. Shall we?"

"Okay," I quipped, "just let me find a seat."

"Oh boy. It's going to be a long afternoon," he said without smiling.

"Yes, it will be," I said with a smile, "if you expect my jokes to be better than that great bit of witticism."

He started to answer but dropped it when he seemed to remember something and got up from his bench, stepped around the table, and slid the bench on my side of his table down a way. "In case you wanted to sit closer and use the table," he explained.

"Oh, nice idea," I said. "Thanks!"

"Okay, let's talk about Oscar," Chuck began, and I was surprised as he regained his seat.

Did he somehow know that Oscar played a truly pivotal role in the start of everything? Not so much later on, maybe, but Oscar did supply the original impetus for the men's group. But even more intriguing to me, did Charles know that I dreamt about Oscar just that last night? "That's ridiculous," I scolded myself. Then I took him back to the beginning of my friendship with Oscar:

"Hi, Epaphras. This is Oscar Rabinowitz from church," I heard, answering my phone on the first Monday morning at home after being in the hospital and then rehab for six months. "I think you might need some help."

"Well, um, hi, Oscar. How are you?" I said, wondering what he meant, and so I asked, "What do you mean? Don't we all need help?"

"I am…okay," he said, answering more frankly than the standard "fine" affords but remaining guarded. "Yes, I am sure that's true enough, but always for some more than others. Listen, I'm sorry to butt in, but I saw you at church yesterday right after the first service and watched you zipping back and forth and all over. I overheard a few bits of the conversations you were having with different people trying to arrange for rides for the week." Oscar was rushing through what seemed like a rehearsed message, and like someone expecting to be shut down right away but very intent on getting it all out. "It seemed like a lot of juggling would be required, and even then, maybe a bunch of contingencies? You were still chasing someone down when I left, but did you get things worked out? Do you feel good about the arrangements? If not, I think I can help."

"I didn't know quite what to think," I told Charles. "I did talk to eight or nine people after the service that morning, and about wore myself out rolling back and forth across the lobby, through the crowd, in and out of the sanctuary, trying to recognize people by their pants, and trying to catch their attention before they left for home. Nobody appreciated the fact that I really just needed a quick answer about their availability so I could scoot back over and keep everyone I was talking to informed and work out a plan. Oscar was right; I heard a lot of 'I'll let you knows' and 'We'll sees.' And too many people wanted to sympathize with me and my legs and my chair and the incredible loss of Teddy all right there and then. I know they were being nice and very sweet, and I needed that too, but just then, I needed to take care of business, so I started feeling frustrated.

"'Maybe the first help I need is to just have someone else who could manage all the crap for me,' I remember thinking, and I began to more fully realize all of the practical problems that would be coming up."

Charles did not hesitate to point out the obvious. "Maybe everybody in the world would want exactly that as well."

"Yes, Charles," I had to admit. "Anyway, by the time I got home from church, I was exhausted and still only had a ramshackle plan for getting to all the appointments coming up that week."

"By the way, Mr. Details, how did you even get to and from church that morning? You must have had something worked out for that, eh?" Chuck asked.

"Not so much me," I answered, "but my sister, Macy, and her husband, Peter, came to town a week earlier to get my house ready for me to come home to from rehab on Thursday. They got my stuff brought down from upstairs and set me up in what was the guest room off the kitchen. A room Teddy used as a prayer room, too, so there was a bulletin board in there with her lists of people and the concerns she prayed about regularly. I kept that there and still look at it every day.

"Macy did a bunch of shopping for me, and she and Pete, excuse me, 'Peter' (he's touchy about his name), moved furniture around to accommodate the wheelchair, lowered stuff from the upper cabinets, etc. They brought me home on Thursday and made sure everything was all set for me to pretty much take care of myself.

"They were there when Wade's company was finishing up the beautiful wheelchair ramp up to the back door for me. Ned was only nineteen or twenty then, but he worked for Wade for a short time before going out on his own, and he did a great job on that project. It still looks brand new and feels as solid as ever."

"What?" I said, reacting because Chuck was giving me a dirty look. "*You* called me 'Mr. Details' so I thought you wanted details! Did I answer the question yet? I don't think so…"

Charles was suddenly exasperated and said, "I don't know! I don't even remember my own question anymore! Something about church, maybe, but I don't even care! Somebody shoot m…" and stopped somewhere in the middle of "me," if that's possible, as he realized the phrase he was about to use might be a little insensitive.

"Then, on Sunday," I went on, unperturbed, "Peter and Macy took me to and from church, to finally answer your question." I had long ago determined not to let my disability interfere with real life. My friends and family, and the guys at MG all knew they could just be themselves and make whatever wisecracks they would normally make around me without worrying about me and my "feelings."

"And I was running around trying to get rides for the week ahead all set up because they had to leave town for home right after lunch," I added, "to answer your next question."

"Don't worry about it. I'm not asking any more questions anymore. You always answer them!"

I ignored him and went on to demonstrate how devastating "feelings" can be if left unchecked. "That was the hardest moment, Chuck, when they left me alone. It struck me first when I realized I couldn't walk out to the driveway with them to say goodbye like people do, before they drove off. I wouldn't have been able to get back up that ramp by myself at that time! So, I sat in the window to watch, but the railing outside was in the way of a good wave, and when I thought I'd open the window to shout my goodbyes, I found out I couldn't reach the latch.

"Even after all the training I had received in rehab, I could not get past the belief that my legs would certainly work if I just tried hard enough! I reached and stretched for that window latch but only from above my hips, and there's just not too much stretch in that limited segment of a guy! I tried so hard that I almost fell out of the chair. Then when I finally gave up and looked out, their rental car was picking up speed as it passed my porch and down the street. I missed the one chance I had at a good wave!

"It was all downhill from that moment, Chuck. I rolled into my new tiny room to have a pity party for myself but did not feel strong enough to lift myself out of the chair, so I just reached my arms out over a pillow, laid my head down, and ended up just bent over the side of my bed, crying. Then the chair slowly rolled backward, dragging my head and arms along the bedspread until I finally thought to lock the brakes! I passed out like that, barely on the bed, and slept in that position for an hour. When I woke up, all the vertebrae I had that could still feel anything at all were in agony! What a mess!"

Chuck looked at me with stupefied sympathy. He

didn't know whether to laugh or feel sorry for me, so he just looked toward me but past me, waiting for the end of the story. I wanted him to look me in the eye. I wanted to look into his eyes, to reach him. So I went on, and I told him how I had called out to God in prayer; actually calling out, like the neighbors were probably wondering what was going on in there. How in my anguish of body, soul, and spirit, God had leaned into my pain and challenged me to put off my sinful nature and to trust Him. I told Chuck that I did not want to. I wanted to keep my sinful nature! That struck me! "I want to keep my sinful nature?" I yelled out loud at the living room walls! But Teddy had picked that light gray color and painted it herself! Now I felt like I was betraying Christ and Teddy too!

Chuck looked up, surprised at where this was going. I thought he might want to defend me from my conviction, which is always a bad idea, so I went on right away to the upside.

"It was that thought that broke me, Charles! The thought of Teddy's being hurt by my attitude brought home to me what I was doing to my Savior, and it broke me good. I cried again, but this time not for myself. I cried out in repentance and sorrow for my attitude. Even a victim can have a sinful attitude.

And I knew that even as I confessed my sin, I was forgiven! For the first time, I truly felt that I was, in fact, buried with Him in baptism and then raised with Him through my faith in the power of God, who raised Jesus from the dead!"

My poor neighbors. If they heard anything from my house, they would have heard me turn from yelling and fighting with God to rejoicing in Him, laughing joyously, and praising Jesus!

"At that point, I was able to get ready for bed the right way. I got myself up on the bed, and after literally pulling my legs out of my pants and shoving them into some pajamas, I went to sleep with joy and in peace!

"Sadly, by the time morning came around, I was right back to worrying about my schedule and my rides, and the weather and if I had enough laundry soap and if Peter and Macy made it home all right and everything else in the world. I needed to spend some real time with God, but instead, I found myself putting that off so I could worry some more. Wow. Can you believe it, Chuck?"

"It does sound kinda stupid," he said, trying, I think, to be supportive.

"Right before the phone rang then, thank you, I

was sitting in that stupid chair (what else could I be doing?) feeling sorry for myself again. I had just dropped some bread into the toaster and pushed the plunger down when I noticed the butter dish was not on the counter. 'I bet I don't have any butter in the house! Macy!'

"Yes, I yelled out loud at my poor little sister who had just given up a precious week of her life to take care of me and stock up my house!

"I was feeling lonely, angry, jealous, slighted, misunderstood, and neglected. Did I mention that I was grieving? And not very well? Yeah, that. And even at the very moment Oscar was offering help, I was tempted to be bitter and judgmental; he reminded me of my sure conclusion that all those people at church yesterday had right then and there decided that they had lives and things to do, just to spite me!

"I started looking around for more things to be upset about and saw the stairway to 'Never Land,' as I was then calling my second floor. I remembered that the very last time I went up those stairs, my legs carried me up two steps at a time, and that was to change my socks because Teddy noticed they didn't match. Of course, it was really because they truly did not match, but I framed it the other way as if to blame Teddy! That again!

"Then I remembered that when I was going through the bag of clothes they had taken off of me at the ER, a few months after the shooting, I found one black and one dark blue sock! I did go up and change my socks that night, but I was so flustered that I took off one mismatched set and put on the other mismatched set! It hit me so hard to realize that the last time I used my legs to climb stairs was just a total waste of leg!"

"A 'waste of leg?'" Chuck said.

"Yes! And Teddy didn't notice the second time, and I can't even tease her for not noticing, and she's not here to laugh at me for 'changing' my socks the way I did, either!

"Oh, I was such a mess, Chuck, and right then, Oscar followed the prompting of God and called me to offer help. The thought of it made me proud and ashamed and embarrassed and joyous all at once. I was a mess, all right, but at just the right time and at just the right place to freely admit to Oscar on the phone that, 'Yes, I do need help.' And went on, humbly, 'What are you suggesting? I could probably use a lot of help.'

EPAPHRAS: THE INTERVIEW

"Even while supposedly admitting I needed help, I was trying to wheel myself into the kitchen, switching the phone from one hand to the other so I could take turns pushing each wheel. I was really just swiveling back and forth, barely gaining any ground. Then I had to wonder if Oscar heard the telltale noise of my neediness when one wheel hit the pantry cabinet while the back of the other wheel banged into the fridge, rattling bottles inside and rocking the junk on top. 'In the house, I'm okay, so far... sorta,' I said, looking up to see if the glass vases still inexplicably stored on the fridge top were going to fall on me or not, 'but getting out and about will be impossible on my own.'

"'Oh good!' Oscar said, and we both quietly ignored the fact that he just celebrated my being unable to get out of the house. 'You know, since Hannah and I were at Drakes that night when your wife was shot...killed, and you were shot and paralyzed, we both somehow felt, we feel like we're part of your family now.' He was talking very slowly, haltingly as he searched for the right words. My ears perked up as his tone became quieter but weightier. 'It's like we have some...very real responsibility. I am sure that sounds strange. I don't know if it makes any sense or not, but is it too much for me to say that we want to…kind of…take care of you?' I could hear the doubt and anxiety in his voice. But also a sincerity and a surety that touched me. My bad thoughts about the church folk melted away. My toast popped up, and my eyes fell on the butter dish where Macy must have placed it on the lowered table, in plain sight, but I didn't even care anymore except to notice that God was, and would be, faithfully meeting all of my real needs.

"I had been in rehab for a long time, and under the great care of good, compassionate professionals. But the sweet, heartfelt words of this guy, who was really only a church acquaintance and way outside of my twenty-something circle, got to me all of a sudden. I couldn't talk! I gaped and choked and gave out with kind of a short, hoarse bellow into the phone. That only embarrassed me and confused poor Oscar, who could not see the tears welling up in my eyes. 'Excuse me?' He said.

"By now, I didn't care if he did hear me cry or whatever I was doing. God was showing me that I needed help. That it was okay to grieve. That there was love in the church. That a version of God's love could be given man to man. I didn't see the whole thing at that moment, but now I know that the whole men's ministry I would come to organize and direct was born just then during and because of that phone call with Oscar.

"I finally managed to say, 'I would be very honored, Oscar, if you could take me around to a couple of places tomorrow. Could you be here a little before 8 a.m.? We would be back here by noon, and I'll make you lunch. Or…we will make lunch together anyway. And then we'll talk about the rest of the week.'

"'That sounds good, Epaphras,' Oscar said, with noticeable joy and relief in his voice. 'I'll see you in the morning!'"

Again, Charles was not impressed. I guess he really did want to be a hard-nosed reporter, so he was achieving that much, anyway. Or was it just me? Was I a true softy? Maybe too sensitive? I guess I don't really know.

Before I made the mistake of broaching that subject with Chuck, who I knew did not want to be my therapist, he asked me for more information about Oscar, so I told him about last night's dream that featured Oscar and then about our first day on the road together, which was twelve years before.

"So glad you asked, Chuck!" I said. "Perhaps it was the long ride home last night, with Barnabas driving so pleasantly and smoothly and with my being so comfortable and stable in my seat, that engendered the dream I had about Oscar. Oscar and Barn were total opposites behind the wheel! I dreamt about the short time, just that one week when I had Oscar driving for me.

"Dreams are weird, but this one was only mildly exaggerated. We were heading out to the cemetery to visit Teddy's grave. That part was real. That's the first place I had Oscar drive me that first day. But in this dream, or nightmare, the car was swerving back and forth across what seemed like a twenty-lane highway at full speed. And at the same time, as we flew side to side, Oscar was driving the gas pedal like a drummer plays the base! Picture it: the car careening back and forth and lurching up and back at the same time! I was holding on to the door and the dashboard and the back of the driver's seat (yes, I know that takes three arms)!

"I have to tell you, Chuck, that his actual driving was truly like that!" Chuck was incredulous. "Well, yes, to a much lesser degree, but still. Oh, and, truth be told, I only have two arms," and I held them up to be counted.

"Yeah, I noticed that much. But oh, I would be

sick! Even at the true, non-dream level," he said emphatically. "What did you do?"

"I was okay in the nausea department," I said. "But it was unnerving and scary. When we first drove away from my house in town, he narrowly missed my neighbor's car parked on the street. I yelled a warning, and without blinking, he simply turned away, easily avoiding the parked car, but then he just about hit an oncoming car! I thought he was playing some kind of a joke! I was trying to listen to him talk, but really, I was only waiting for the punchline. Then we hit the two-lane out of town. There he just kept going across the line on each side of the highway. And pumping his foot on the gas pedal down and up and down and up."

"So, did he get over it? Was he overtired or something that morning?" Chuck wanted to know.

"No, it just kept up, and I found out that was the way he always drove! He never did hit anything and did not need me to warn him that he was getting too close to one side or the other, I found out. I think he 'averaged' a perfectly straight line down the road."

"So, you just got used to it?"

"Yes and no," I said. "You see, the whole time he was talking. Telling me about his wife, Hannah, and with an amazing nonchalance that did not at all correlate with the driving. Finally, I was convinced that he really drove like that and that he was so focused on his love and concern for Hannah and her needs that he didn't even consciously notice that he was winding all over the map.

"I found the best way to use my arms to grip the car and brace myself. My legs weren't of any use, as they were only flopping back and forth. In the end, I found that I could actually listen and focus on Oscar's Plight, as I came to call it, and we ended up having some important discussions over the next couple of days."

Charles' eyes locked strangely on mine. I had pulled my chair up to the table just a minute before, and we were not too far apart. His eyes held my attention. "Oh wow," Chuck said. "You had some 'important discussions.'" He did not look happy. "How am I supposed to write an intriguing article out of that? I don't know what I'm going to do with this." While he was making this surprising objection and maintaining solid eye contact, he was dramatically shuffling in his seat and flailing one arm over his head, and at the same time, he slipped an envelope out from under his notebook and pushed it under his palm across the table right into my hand.

I had been randomly moving about the room since we began the interview, but just then, I was parked right across from Chuck and had my hands in front of me on the table. When I saw what he was doing, I realized that the camera was directly behind me and that our hands were out of its view, and I quickly decided to play along.

"Interesting," I thought as I put the envelope into the inside coat pocket while trying not to move my upper arm and shoulder. And I played along with his bad acting by contributing my own: "What do you want me to say? He hit a cow and rolled the car? The story is what it is, Mr. Charles! This whole thing was your idea!" And a whole swarm of thoughts flew through my head at once.

- The envelope sliding nicely into the pocket of my coat triggered a memory. I couldn't help but mouth the words "man pocket." Teddy always referred to such a pocket that way, and I always thought it was so cute. Now I do the same. And apparently, no matter what the circumstances.

- The warden must be listening, and Charles is concerned about what was said in here. But what was the sensitive part? I thought Charles' eruption had more to do with the propinquity of our hands on the table than with the talk about Oscar. He must have prepared the envelope and planned for its transfer well before our meeting today.

- Would there be any trouble getting the note, as I assumed there to be in the envelope, out of the prison? They took my phone and other stuff coming in, but would they have some reason, or excuse, to search me on the way out today? They didn't yesterday.

- And then it occurred to me that I now know what Jim Phelps felt like just before a commercial break when his Impossible Mission Force was possibly about to be unveiled by the bad guys. Then again, I probably had more in common with Maxwell Smart. Except that he had his 99 to back him up, and my Teddy was not there.

"What are you saying, Chuck? Do you want to hear about Hannah and Oscar or not? It truly is one of the great love stories of our time!"

"Love story?" he asked, softening and brightening a little. "I thought they were older."

"Oh, brother." Now it was my turn to at least act

frustrated. "What are you saying about older people?"

"Okay, okay. Nothing! How about a break?" he asked. "I could sure use one."

"Yeah. I'll just get a drink of water, anyway."

When Chuck got up and knocked on the door, I saw the guard step right over to open it, and I suddenly realized he could easily have seen the envelope being transferred across the table if he had been looking in the right direction at the right time. I was so busy thinking about the camera that I forgot about the window! Oh, brother, indeed! And I had compared myself to Jim Phelps!

All the times in the past when I thought I was so cleverly hiding my sin came to mind. Like the time I thought no one could see me stealing Life Savers from the candy rack in the grocery store just because I grabbed them from the back side. I was only four, but still; I might have realized that I was not invisible back there or that Mom might wonder where I got candy when she was the sole manager of all my finances at the time. Every sin, in and of itself, is, by definition, a failure. Doesn't it follow that more failures should be inherently connected to the original failures? There is no such thing as the perfect crime because there's no such thing as a quality sinner. "Even if the warden misses something on his monitor, God doesn't," I told myself. And then I felt really tired. Was it the sleep of the guilty I'd heard about? "I wonder if I overthink things," I thought.

Anyway, I was relieved to see that the guard at the door was Krispy! Of course, then I had to wrestle not only with the ethics of hiding the note Charles gave me but possibly the ethics of involving Kris in any subterfuge. I finally decided that since Chuck and I were meeting explicitly in order to communicate with each other, and since that's essentially all that happened, we were fine. We just happened to decide, all of a sudden, that part of our communication would actually be kept private instead of supposedly private. And if I were to be searched on the way out and accused of something nefarious, then I would have to deal with that claim there and then.

While Charles was gone to the secure restroom, Kris and I talked about the church softball team's prospects without his great skills and leadership on the field since he would be moving closer to the prison.

"Your guys will be fine without me, Epps," he tried to assure me. "Especially because my new church's team will be way over here in Riverside, and you'll never have to play against me!"

"Promise?" I said. "I'd like to see that in writing. But who will take your place at shortstop? Oh, it doesn't matter. We have fun, and it's good for everyone to hang out with each other like that in the summer."

"Sure!" Kris said. "Now that I won't be helping your team win the championship, the whole thing 'doesn't matter' anymore, and it's just good to 'hang out'! I see how it is, Epaphras!"

I ignored his analysis and changed the subject with a wink and a smile.

"Hey, will you be the one 'walking' me out again today? I think Barn is hoping to say hi this time." And the note in my pocket felt like a big lump that Kris was intensively scrutinizing!

"It looks that way. I hope so, I'd like to see him too, but I just do what I'm told." Krispy somehow failed to notice the giant bulge pulsating through my coat!

"Understood."

Charles came out just then with his standard wet collar look and walked over. "Ready to tell me some more boring stories?" he said, rolling his eyes and making a gagging face at Kris, who smiled despite all of his training and opened the door for us.

"That's what I heard," Kris allowed as the door closed shut, and Chuck and I both glanced at the camera, waiting for us to sit down.

"Well, I had mentioned that there was a love story about Oscar and Hannah coming up next, but it might just disappoint."

"Oh?" Chuck said.

"Well, yes, they shared a very deep love," I said. "The very best kind, in fact, but nothing like the Hollywood version full of romance and sex and laughter and poignant eye contact."

"Not sure what you mean, Epps."

"Well, it's probably too much to get into now, Chuck, but let me put it this way. Oscar loved Hannah…despite Hannah. After they fell in love and got married, and had a few exciting years, the seeds that were sewn into her life as the daughter of a very abusive man began to germinate. When a child is mistreated—called names, insulted, beaten, or even assaulted—the damage runs deep and deeply impacts her growth and even her ability to mature wholly.

"Oscar found that his love could not be readily

returned but was swallowed up. He said it was like watering a garden in the desert. The refreshment might brush by the plant stem on its way to the roots and create some hope, but it would mainly go into the ground and rush right by the roots, too, disappearing into the dry sand deep below.

"A good mother and father *nurture* their child. They prepare him to receive and retain and relish whatever good love comes their way in life, starting with the love of God.

"Anyway. Oscar's love for Hannah did that nurturing work for her, eventually. It takes much longer for an adult than for a child because it's not so much building from the ground up as it is demolition and remodeling that's required for the adult. But that steady, committed love did, in fact, ready Hannah to welcome and embrace the love of God in her heart, which made all the difference…eventually!

"Someday, we will talk about their story. Or better yet, maybe you'll be out and get to meet them for yourself! Then you can hear about the flat tire, and the eighty-three cents, and the smile!"

"So, you're really not gonna tell me now?" Chuck objected.

"Naaah. I got you on the hook, so I'm satisfied," I

told him and laughed out loud!

"But we have plenty of time. My battery is good, six gigs of memory available, bathroom break is done, and temperature and humidity are fine in here. Let's go. I don't have all day." Chuck quickly looked away from me and studied his notes at this seeming contradiction, and I let it go. But his changing moods and impatience made me wonder all the more about the contents of my pocket. I so wanted to just take it out and read it! And I began to wonder if Charles really had a future in journalism. His bedside manner, or whatever they call it down at the newspaper or TV studio, was atrocious!

"So, you really want to hear a love story, eh, Charles?" I probed a little.

"Actually, it's not that part so much, but what you said about her father hurting her. I can relate. My dad was very rough with me too. Maybe that's why I'm in here today," he said, looking sadly at his orange jumpsuit and the block walls and locked door. "So, I do want to hear how Hannah overcame. She did, right? I sure do hope so!"

"Yes, Charles, she certainly did. She—" And he cut me off. "That's all I need to know right now, Epaphras. Thanks. If you still want to do this, I'll be better prepared to continue on Tuesday. And I'll keep my personal life out of it."

"I hope you don't do *that*!" I said. "You need more than what a professional, sterile style guide can give you to write a valuable article. Your personal empathy and understanding are what will make the whole thing real to your reader," throwing in the little "singular" jab to relieve his tension just then. Chuck caught it and gave me a grunt as he stood up to knock on the door. "I guess there's a balance in there somewhere. I only hope my *one* reader appreciates my efforts," he said, but I noticed he did not smile or even roll his eyes as he glanced over at me.

"Hey, we do still have some time on the clock. If you want, I would love to simply share the gospel message with you, my friend. I came to the prison in the first place just to do that and never really did. Are you up for that?"

"Oh dang, I already knocked on the door!" he said like a wise guy and shrugged at me helplessly. "Maybe I'll hear it when you tell me Hannah's story. I think it's interwoven, isn't it?"

He *was* listening! "Yes. Yes, it is," I said happily as we both saw the guard through the window.

When the door popped open and Chuck quickly

disappeared, a qualifying phrase he had used a minute earlier finally registered with me. I think I had heard him say, "*If* you still want to do this." "What was that supposed to mean?" I wondered and thought again of the note that had been burning a hole in my pocket all afternoon. "Now I don't even want to look at it."

CHAPTER 7

THE SMALL TALK

And so, I didn't. Nor did any of the guards inspect my pocket and neither did a note-sensing alarm go off at the gate. I was finally in the clear to read the note, but oddly, uninterested. Or maybe afraid to look.

Krispy did push me out, and he did get a few minutes to talk to Barny, but I was too distracted to engage in the banter. They must have noticed my mood, so they cut it short, and we headed home. I left Barn alone to drive and pray and stop at whatever fast food drive-throughs he wanted. I couldn't even eat. Too busy wrestling with too many questions.

After a brief but decent night's sleep, I was regretting my reluctance to read Charles' note right away. The curiosity started itching me first thing Saturday morning. But I had men's group at six o'clock and had to get ready and be there early for the couple of guys who might come in ahead of the scheduled time to chat privately. I decided, if Barn was willing, to go to Drakes after the meeting, and I would read the note there over breakfast. What could go wrong? Other than Greg, that is.

Lo and behold, Greg was the first one to walk into the men's group meeting room! For all of his previous boasting about being the champion of early risers, he had continued to come in at the last minute over these past few months of recent involvement and always in such a disheveled state. So when he walked in so early, and looking all fresh and ready for the day, I was doubly astounded. Then he surprised me again by confronting me with the most blatant and hurtful questions!

Typically, Greg sat alone in the back of the room. He always paid close attention, it seemed, to every conversation in the room, and yet barely participated in the study I led, and he never contributed to the group discussion. But last Saturday, when he and I were the only ones in the room, he walked right over, put his hands on the armrests of my wheelchair and leaned over me.

"How are you Epaphras? Time for a new wheelchair I see. Are there any new developments in the death of your wife? Are the police even thinking about her anymore?"

THE SMALL TALK

People our age should not get that close to each other. I know I was aging. At thirty-eight this year, I could feel it, even if it was only in half of my body. My lower half was pain-free, but the upper half did not feel good. Nor did aging look good on Greg. We are the same age, but even with his supposedly superior health regimen, I could see in a second that, up close, he exuded a strong impression of stress-filled aging. The minor wrinkles were multiplying. The nose and ear hairs were establishing a strong front, and with his being so close, I noticed a small gang of eyebrow hairs that escaped the trimmer. The gray roots at Greg's hairline, though very short, were evidence of an ongoing battle. Even before he got to the part about Teddy's death, I was thinking, "Let it go already."

But that last question hit me hard, and I automatically recoiled! Without thinking, I reached up and pushed him away from me and out of my space! The wheels on my chair were locked, and it rocked backward momentarily when I shoved, and I shouted, "What the heck, Greg? Where do you get off?"

"I'm sorry!" he was saying. "I am sorry. I didn't think." I knew he wouldn't hit me—a guy in a wheelchair—for pushing him like that, but neither did I expect him to virtually shrink and cower away from me—a guy in a wheelchair—as he did.

We both heard footsteps and voices on the porch outside the door. Greg stood himself up straighter, brushed his hair back, and straightened his shirt. The door opened, and Ned walked in with Isaac. "You think you're sick of seeing *me* every day? I'm *really* sick of seeing *you* all the time!" Isaac was saying as they came inside, laughing. Greg looked at his watch and said, "Oh yeah! I have to be somewhere else right now," and walked out the door without looking at any of us.

Isaac seemed taken aback and looked at me. "I wasn't talking about *him*, Epps!"

"I know, Isaac. It's all good," I said, going on duty. "How are you two comrades getting along? Almost done with that garage you've been building for the past six months?" I asked.

"Six months!" Ned said. "We finished it yesterday, and wasn't it more like six days, Isaac?"

"Five. We started framing on Monday."

"So, I got sick of working with you in just one week?" Ned had to bait him again. "That's a new record!"

And everything was back to normal. At least for

everyone else in the room. I made it through the meeting, leaving most of the heavy lifting of the discussion based on Colossians 3 to my partners.

We had been slowly going through the section that some editor titled "Rules for Christian Households" for a while, and I was glad for the reminder that I was "working for the Lord, not for men"! I wasn't there for Greg, per se, or anyone else, but "it is the Lord Christ you are serving," Paul said!

And then, enabling me to go on through the day with peace, was the final verse: "Anyone who does wrong will be repaid for his wrong." God would ultimately mete out all the rewards and punishments warranted in perfect order one day, and I could let it all go at that! Praise God!

Barn had no plans for after the meeting except for getting me home, so he was glad to take me down to Drakes and have a late breakfast with me.

It was just a couple of days past the actual anniversary date, July 12, but we were married on a Saturday after all so this would be our "even week" anniversary. As of Thursday evening, it had been fifteen years since Teddy and I were married, thirteen years since Teddy was killed and I was paralyzed, and about eleven since the men's group began. It had been such a long time, so as we were going into Drakes that morning, I thought I could handle whatever feelings the confluence of anniversaries might bring up. I should have known better.

Possibly, if Barnabas had stayed with me, it would have been okay, but as soon as he pushed me to a table, not *the* table, but one from which I could look over at *the* table and the whole area where Teddy and I were sitting that night, Barn noticed that the now twenty-three-year-old Queenie was taking off her apron and looking like she was about to leave, so he abandoned me and rushed over to say hi. I was suddenly left to struggle by myself to move a four-legged chair out of the way to make room for my wheeled version.

Barn found out that Queenie had been looking for a ride to pick up her car at a repair shop, so naturally, Barnabas jumped at the chance and volunteered to help her out. When he asked me, like a kid asking his dad for more ride tickets at the fair, if I minded his leaving for a bit and how long I expected to be there, I told him I would be fine for a couple of hours, so he should go ahead.

Then Queenie came over to say hi and to thank me for lending Barnabas out for what had suddenly increased, in her words, to a "few" hours! I was glad, actually, for some time alone with my thoughts, imagining fantastically that I had full control over my circumstances, even while I was suddenly realizing that I had lost control over when Barn would be back to take me home!

I had been in Drakes a lot over the years and had watched Queenie grow up in the business and into a very capable and beautiful young woman. She looked great in her slick black hostess outfit and with her light blonde hair collected nicely in a long ponytail. Several of the young guys at church, including Barnabas, had their eye on her since she started attending a few years earlier, and anybody could see why. I was glad that he had the opportunity to step up and act on his interest.

Queenie always had my attention as well but for a different reason. I still saw her as that ten-year-old girl who was so enthralled by Teddy's sweet spirit at our table that last night. I was struck when I realized that she was now about the same age that Teddy was when she died, and on top of that, Queenie was, in fact, the last person Teddy poured herself into! I always felt that a part of Teddy was still in there, and that made her very special to me.

I know better, of course. Teddy could, and did, always influence those around her, especially anyone open to being loved and moved. But she was not the Holy Spirit. Only He can truly inhabit, empower, enable, and comfort those open to His super influence like Teddy was. When I looked for Teddy in Queenie, I was really watching to see if some of the same Fruit of the Spirit might be accruing in her life.

All that being said, I found myself feeling jealous of Barnabas that day because, way down deep, it truly felt like he was about to go out with my Teddy!

I actually went into Drakes with Oscar that first week I was back in town after rehab, maybe seven months after the shooting. We had come back from the cemetery visit, and I was so anxious to get my feet, or wheels, on the ground that I had him pull over all of a sudden when I saw an open parking spot in front of the restaurant instead of going another ten minutes to my house as we had planned. I was so glad to get off the road and out of that car! The mental process of adjusting from Oscar's "Tilt-A-Whirl" car ride to my rolling chair was not easy, but at least then I could drive myself, and I may even have been a little bit rude when I shooed Oscar away from the chair, and bade him to get the door instead of pushing.

That simple delight did not last too long, however. Poor little Queenie, still maybe only ten and a half at that time, was just inside, and when she saw me for the first time in months and rolling in so awkwardly in that brand new shiny wheelchair, she screamed, dropped a sheaf of paper place mats, and burst into tears! And then she didn't know what to do or which way to turn. She wanted to hug me, or maybe to be hugged by me, but she was afraid, and I wasn't Teddy, and Teddy was gone, and I was so unused to being in a wheelchair I didn't know what to do for her either.

She ran to her dad, who was going by with a tray of drinks balanced over his head. He only brushed her off, as was his way, with a loud bark as he glanced my way and nodded professionally. Her mom, who was always known simply as Updike, was in her wheelchair too, of course, and they knew how to manage a hug around it, but Updike only wanted to see how I was doing, so the crying child registered yet another, this time unexpected, rejection. Her frustration called up more tears, but they seemed to go underground, swallowed, and threatening to swallow her.

I knew that Updike would be the one person this week who would not ask me if the shooter had been identified yet, as if the answer to that question would not have been broadcast repeatedly every hour on the hour if someone had been picked up and charged. But she was sure to ask me a deeper, probing question about my recovery or my faith or my walk with God or about something much more important than the mere satisfaction of justice. I didn't want to answer any of those questions just then, either.

I tried, rudely, to turn away from Updike before she could query my very soul as she was wont to do, but I rotated in the wrong direction as if it was my first day in a wheelchair and got even more flustered. Just then, she was fortuitously called away by a customer complaining about a lack of ranch dressing at the salad bar, so I caught a break and was able to figure out my chair again.

The loudest part of Queenie's crying petered out, and I noticed that she had run into the open waitstaff area. I saw her there sobbing quietly but deeply and desperately clinging to the rigid and sticklike Zoe who had her weeping-willow arms draped loosely over Queenie's heaving back. Zoe stood there like a statue in the park, patting Queenie perfunctorily but with her eyes focused on me! The incongruity struck me, and I felt a chill; the cold and calculating Zoe staring at me so intently from across the room while only passively offering whatever

THE SMALL TALK

comfort the little girl could glean from her stony bony facade. The contrast with Teddy was stark and shocking. It made me miss my Teddy all the more, and I almost prayed to her instead of to Jesus. "What should I do?"

Oscar was oblivious to the ruckus my mere presence had brought to the place. He had gone ahead in and made a path for me, and after moving one chair out of the way to make room for my wheelchair at the table, he sat down with a menu. I guess Queenie's crying was the only outward sign of mayhem in the restaurant, so as that subsided, a pleasant but awkward hush fell over the room.

Inwardly, however, I was a mess. Coming through that front entry had stirred up so much trouble in my mind. I had heard that the old front door had been quickly removed after the shooting and that a modern set of double doors had been installed. And at first, I could admire the changes.

There was more than just a new door. I saw a whole new entry area with more waiting room and a fancy maître d' stand, which looked great. But my mind suddenly turned inside out, and the current condition of the room on that cold day in February 2000 faded away and was replaced by a nightmarish rendition of the scene as it might have been on last summer's July 12.

I saw splintered wood and broken glass and bright red blood, and I heard screams and rushing feet. In my mind's eye, there were dozens of bullet holes in the walls and furniture. I was only sure of Queenie's crying and Zoe's stare. The rest of my thoughts were bouncing all over, and I couldn't keep up.

I thought I recognized the booth where Yeti and Ralphie had been wrangling that night. And all of a sudden, Yeti was sitting there with blood on *his* face. He noticed me, and with a look of horror, he pointed at me and fainted!

Then there was Oscar reaching across his table behind Teddy with a saltshaker and salting Hannah's plate for her. "Just the way you like it," he was saying, "Just the way you like it," as she stared at the plate with glassy eyes.

I saw "our" table over by the bar and found myself wondering stupidly if it was still wet and if people can use wet cash.

Behind everything else, I heard a staccato, tapping rhythm and finally realized it was the sound of Teddy's rapid footsteps heading across the hardwood floor toward that fateful door, and I started to shout

out loud, "Stop! I'm sorry!" but bit my tongue and all that came out was a weak "don't."

Then my real eyes fell on Zoe back in the shadows again, and instead of being concerned for the sway she was gaining over Queenie, I wondered whatever had happened to my steak dinner. Did she eat it herself and owe me one? Was it put in the fridge that night, and might it still be waiting for my return? I knew it was all ridiculous, but my visions only got worse!

I saw Greg's truly handsome face turn sinister and appear before me, all twisted and winking. I felt the need to scream at him, or somebody, or anybody. But could not. All at once, then, I wanted to cry as Queenie had, and like Queenie, maybe I was even scared and desperate enough to pretend I could find comfort with Zoe's flaccid arms propped around *me*.

With that repugnant idea, I came to my senses! I closed my eyes tightly, trying to squeeze all of those scenes out of my mind, especially the last one!

Then I stirred myself and wheeled hastily over to the table by Oscar, where he sat hungrily weighing options in the menu and glanced up to say, "Hey do you want to split an appetiz—" I interrupted him to say, "Let's get out of here," and started pushing myself back toward the horrid new doorway we had just come through, though it felt like we had been there for hours. It took a moment, but when Oscar realized I was serious and came hurrying up behind me to grab and take control of my chair, I abruptly stopped dead and spun around, saying, more to myself than to Oscar, "Can't do it. Back way." As I turned in front of him, he slammed into my knees, lost his balance, and fell forward, spinning me back around to where I could readily watch one of his flailing arms push a full glass of water and a plate of steak fries from a table into a lady's lap, before his full body fell flat on the floor with an "oomph"! I couldn't help him up or do anything for him even if I was inclined to, which I wasn't, so I just turned around again and wheeled myself to the back door and waited for him to catch up and open it. It wasn't long. He hobbled up with a gimp and a grimace. I thought he was bleeding, but he was just spreading ketchup back and forth between his face and his coat sleeves. As soon as we were out in the cold, I realized I had left my gloves inside, but when Oscar offered, reluctantly but bravely, to go back inside for them, I would not let him. "I always lose something at Drakes," I said. "It's my thing."

Now this visit, in 2012, after so many years of

recovery and healing and successful ministry, started out much differently. First of all, I am so happy to report the now twenty-three-year-old Queenie did not cry when she saw me. She gave me a big smile, in fact, which only brightened noticeably when Barnabas came over from the restroom, all ready to go. Queenie exhibited all the niceties a well-versed restaurant manager practiced every day with her customers. She was much better at it than Drake ever was and almost as good as her mom, the ever-sincere and personable hostess, "Updike."

Queenie really was running the place now. In fact, when Zoe, her long-ago mentor, passed by with a tray full of entrees, Queenie directed her to get me whatever I might need at no charge. Zoe stiffened with those instructions and looked at me sternly but answered her new boss with the proper "Okay."

Barnabas and Queenie ran through all the polite small talk they could muster as quickly as possible, said goodbye, and went out laughing through the same good old back door Oscar and I used for our miserable retreat so long ago. I watched them, smiling, and thought, "This could get interesting; I know that Krispy likes Queenie too."

CHAPTER 8

THE QUESTION

I had turned my chair almost all the way around to watch the kids go out and over to my car. I saw that Barnabas surprised Queenie by going around to open the door for her, acting all chivalrous and over-the-top. She seemed to like the little dose of kindness and let him serve her graciously as he made sure her feet were all the way in before closing the door. Barn was apparently so pleased with himself and giddy about the chance to spend time with Queenie that when he hastily skipped around the front of the car, he misjudged his skills and banged his shin into the bumper!

I saw Queenie cover her mouth and then lean over to open the driver's door for him from the inside. Barn hobbled around the door, mumbling, and if I know Barnabas, he was telling God that He was right about "pride going before the fall."

Groaning for him, as I could certainly remember

the good old days when I could run into things and hurt myself, and chuckling sweetly, too, as I thought about how endearing such a moment could be for a wannabe couple on their first outing. Teddy always liked to remind me of the time I had been boasting about how well I could handle cold weather, but then I had to have her "rescue" me one winter evening after a dinner date when I was full of ice-cold lemonade and started shivering as we strolled in a park among the Christmas decorations. "Should I get you into my car and warm you up, Ernest Shackleton?" she teased. And all I could say was "Y-e-e-s, p-p-p-lea-ease!" Oh, she got a lot of mileage out of that exchange!

"What do you want?" Zoe said suddenly and loudly. My left arm reached so fast for the hand rim on my chair that I smacked my knuckles on the edge of the table before I was able to find the wheel and get the chair under control. Then I spun around so fast that my left foot fell off its footrest and wedged under the right footrest. I knew that would have hurt a lot if I could feel anything at all down there, so just by visualizing the ankle skin scrape up in a pile, and by faith alone, I was able to empathetically produce a good "Ouch!"

Zoe was not standing beside the table, pad in

hand and pen at the ready like a good waitress would be, surprise, surprise, but she was sitting in the chair across from me, and she did not even have an order pad within reach! She ignored my faux pain and my consternation and only repeated, "*What* do you want?"

"Well, I don't want you to scare the crap out of me like that! What do you want to do *that* for?" I shot back, embarrassed, and looking at my skinned knuckles like maybe I should take them to the ER. "Wow, Zoe! I don't even have a menu yet anyway."

"I mean, what do you want *here*? Why do you keep coming here, even after this place killed… what's her name?"

I was stunned. Did she really just say "What's her name"? That hurt more than the hand and even how I imagined the ankle would be feeling, and I made a mental note to look at it later and tend to whatever was damaged. Many problems can occur, and much injury be done without the benefit of pain sounding an alarm.

I stared at Zoe while my befuddled mind started hunting for an answer to give her. It had all kinds of ungodly ideas; complaints, accusations, even insults, and angry outbursts were nominated. But it came up with nothing worthy of breath or born of righteousness. Nothing concrete or civil. Nothing especially that would impact or truly affect Zoe at all. Certainly, nothing "wrapped in forgiveness," as Teddy would often say, came to mind.

Slowly, I said only, "I want a double Drake burger. With everything. No fries. Salad. Thousand Island. *That's* what I want. And lemonade. Raspberry lemonade. Quarter cup ice," I added, with ever-diminishing dramatic effect.

I never knew Zoe to be one of those amazing waitresses who can take the orders from a table full of people all at once and memorize all of the particulars in a flash, but she at least acted like she had my simple order straight in her mind when she popped up and strode swiftly away to the kitchen. I saw her swipe a napkin from the nearest table as she went by it, and I figured she was probably hoping to find a pen and the chance to write down what I ordered before she forgot and had to come crawling back to ask again.

Perhaps Zoe also remembered that her boss, Queenie, would be on my side and, maybe after today, even eternally indebted to me for setting her up with a new husband, Barnabas, and was afraid this little escapade would be reported to her. Zoe didn't have to worry about me that way. I've always believed it's better to keep things close, between stakeholders, as it were, and not to share private interactions without a great need.

As the double doors to the kitchen swung shut behind Zoe, I asked myself, "What else can happen?" and blew out a long stream of burden. Sometimes I would symbolically "cast all my anxiety upon Him" that way. And I would then take in the rest of the lovely verse like a deep inhalation of fresh, promise-filled, encouraging air: "…because He cares for you." "Thank You, Lord!" I said aloud but quietly and looked up to see one of the other staff coming out with my salad. "That was fast!" I said to the guy, with a smile. Apparently, judging by his wet apron, he was a dishwasher. He looked at me curiously and, without saying a word, dropped my food in front of me like it was a dirty platter splashing into the sink. "Yup. Dishwasher," I confirmed my guess.

After thanking God for another meal and asking him to bless Zoe in whatever way she really needed, I began to munch on the salad and to seriously think about Zoe's question. "What *do* I want here?" Or "Why *do* I keep coming in here?" This would take some processing.

EPAPHRAS: THE INTERVIEW

First, I tried to separate the question itself, which was all about me, from Zoe's apparent angst and self-centered interest in my staying away from her. "I certainly understood the roots of that! That's all Lenny's fault!" I mused and smiled at the thought of telling him so when he came by next weekend with a load of manure for my garden.

CHAPTER 9

THE REFUGE

Poor Zoe. She was the oldest of three sisters but had one brother, Lenny, who was one year older than her. Lenny wanted a brother so badly but kept getting sisters! By the time he was eight and his load of chores on the family farm was starting to chafe, he realized it was only going to get worse.

Zoe was born selfish, and by the time she was twelve, she was entirely bent on staying out of the barn. It wasn't the barn, necessarily, as it was the work being done in the barn that Zoe was so anxious to avoid. She learned early on how to manipulate her dad to that end. Worse, she made sure Lenny knew that she knew she was getting away with murder and that he could not do anything about it! She loved to whip him into a frenzy of anger and hate and then wait for him to explode and get into trouble when he took it out on the animals or equipment.

But the worst thing happened next. Instead of

responding to Zoe's behavior with the opposite, good behavior, Lenny unexpectedly found that his inclination was to respond in kind. With practice, he became as mean or meaner than Zoe. And he did not limit his rage against the one, but he became an ogre to all of his little sisters.

Like a prison guard or nursing home caregiver whose diligence over the needs of his charges sometimes devolves from careless to callous to cruel, Lenny went from being degrading to disdainful to despiteful of everyone around him.

Enter Epaphras, the dorky, skinny high school kid with the weirdest name anyone ever heard.

I had never even been to a farm before that first time in June of '89, but my mom thought it would be good for me, and she knew that Mr. Palmer was ready to admit he needed another "man" to help him out. I was nervous that first day but excited, too, until I met, or "felt," this new Lenny.

Of course, I knew nothing about all the family intrigue at the time. And admittedly, I only have Lenny's side of the story now. An unrepentant Zoe would not be able to describe, let alone recognize, such things. Nor would she ever want to. So, it was Lenny himself who told me, much later, how much he resented my being there. Even though he hated the burden of work he had to carry, he felt threatened by the possible comparisons that might develop between our work performances. He placed all his hope in keeping me down, so he loved the fact that I was that weird kid a year behind him in school with the extremely oddball name! He knew he could and would take full advantage of the opportunity to "give me gall," as he put it. And he did.

I've already said that I had grown used to dealing with people who just plain didn't care if they were hurting others, but Lenny took it to a whole new extreme. And I was in his hands, as it were. I was his charge. Lenny's father gave him the duty to train me and coach me in my new chores. And Lenny took that as his commission to berate and harass me without mercy and without end.

My dad must have had some idea of how this might go because he made sure to get alone with me several times that spring and gave me some great insights about patience and endurance and about what it means to love your enemies. I listened and nodded my head a lot and said, "Of course. The stuff that Jesus would do. I get it." But then Dad went on to say, "I don't think you do. But I want you to be ready to get it when you need it." That, I didn't get. Until Lenny was beating me up virtually every day, and I suddenly found myself thinking of him as a real "enemy"! As soon as that word appeared in my thoughts, I began to "get" the importance of the attitude my dad wanted me to take. He wanted me to endure by forgiving.

I was such a wimp before I started to actually make my body work all day that summer! Not that I knew it. I thought I had an active life, but only because I sometimes goofed around with sports. My friends and I played softball sometimes and shot a basketball around a lot, so we thought we were jocks. After moving hay bales around for a few weeks, I began to realize what it means to work at something; what a real athlete or a real dancer or a real farmer must do to excel.

Considering how Lenny assailed me every day with the verbal abuse, I did not even think about what was happening to my body. But by the fourth of July, I noticed that my hands were tougher, and I had a classic farmer's tan; dark face and neck and forearms, but if you saw me without a shirt on, you might think I was indeed wearing a white T-shirt! I realized all at once that I was able to manhandle a hay bale, and I could push hard enough against a cow to swing her backside out of my way to get in between two cows at the milking station. The milking equipment itself got lighter and easier to manipulate, and my shirts got tighter. My mom said she thought I was getting heavier and taller too, but I brushed that off as part of her mom-love lore. I did take notice, though, when my little sister Macy said that her friends said I was almost beginning to start to become good-looking!

Anyway, I was so glad to be getting in shape for the rigorous demands of work on the farm as well as quickly learning the tasks I was required to perform every day. I wanted to do the work so well, if only to make sure that my weird name was the only "legitimate" thing Lenny could use against me. And on that front, I was even getting used to Lenny's steady stream of disses. That is to say, I was getting good at totally shutting out his voice.

Then one day in the middle of August, I was thinking about school starting up again but couldn't decide if I was happy or sad about leaving the farm routine. Even with Lenny's incessant badgering routine considered, I would miss the exercise and the overall satisfaction that came with the hard work.

I was thinking about it when I walked up on the house porch to go in for lunch—a full dinner, really—and overheard Zoe through the screen door. She was picking on Lenny as he washed his hands in the kitchen sink by calling him Leonard and with the silliest singsong teasing voice. I heard her threaten to tell "that hunky Mr. Epaphras" how much Lenny hated his "real" name if he didn't promise to wash all the dishes after we had done the afternoon milking and I was gone.

Lenny raised his voice and started to say, "You better not! An' I ain't washing your dishes ever aga—" but stopped when he turned and saw that I was coming toward the door. But instead of opening the screen door just then, I stopped short to scratch my ankle and then found I had to retie my boots. I had seen the look of horror on Lenny's face when he saw me as he realized the fullness of an evil trifecta; 1) He had been hassling me all morning like a champion, 2) Zoe liked me more than him, and 3) he knew I heard about the name and the apparently ongoing blackmail scheme.

I could have buried him right then and there.

But I still thought Zoe was meaner than Lenny, so I wasn't about to take her side. I had seen her in action before. So, when I went into the kitchen, I pretended to both of them that I didn't hear anything and even provided a subject that was sure to distract Zoe from going forward on this topic. "Oh, Zoe! I thought you were your mom standing there. You look great!" Most fourteen-year-old girls don't want to be mixed up with their mothers, maybe, but Lenny, in his infinite interest in disparaging everyone around him, had once let me know, in so many words, that Zoe was frustrated with the dearth in her figure and jealous of her mother's! It worked. Zoe gave me a profuse "thank you!" and somehow managed to even blush a little before she took off to find a full-length mirror as the rest of the family came into the room.

Lenny didn't know what to do. Or say. We sat down to eat, and for once, the younger sisters had the chance to run the conversation because Lenny was actually thinking about something. Zoe had meandered back into the room quietly, looking confused and disappointed, and sat down without picking up her fork and without looking at me. I succeeded in saving Lenny, I guess, but at the cost of hurting Zoe terribly. Maybe *I* was the meanest one in the room.

An hour later, Lenny had still not said a word while we worked in the tool shed together. Mr. Palmer had plans to renovate the space, and we were told to sort the old junk tools and useless parts from what might actually be of some value to the farm. I found some discs and put them in the "keep" pile. Lenny noticed and said, "Those are from three models ago, at least, you…" and his voice dropped off. "Scrap pile."

"Oh. Okay," I said and started moving them again. "You know…" *Crash!* Went one heavy old disc onto the hill of scrap steel we had started building. "I would kill…" *Clang! Clash!* Went two more. "…for a name as normal as…" *Clank!* "…Leonard."

It's amazing what one good moment can do for a relationship, and to a life. I did not know it then, but Lenny desperately needed to know how to forgive! My unsought forgiveness, also unknown and unplanned for by me, acted as a catalyst of conviction. In that instant, he knew and admitted how wrongfully he had been acting toward me and toward his sisters and even toward his family at large by being so lax in his work.

Sadly, and here I am actually getting back to the point, as Lenny right away began to practice forgiving Zoe, Zoe practiced taking even more advantage of her brother. She did not get it.

By seventeen, she had had enough of Leonard and

his stupid sweet spirit. She could see that he would eventually be taking over the farm and figured she had better get away from him and it and everything that she found so annoying at home. Zoe did not want to be "forgiven," and she most certainly did not want to be challenged into being forgiving! She had to get away.

Even when Zoe was only sixteen, she tried to get Yeti interested in her, not caring that he was six years older, nor was she at all bothered by the fact that he was already married to Ralphie! But even the old Yeti already knew the kind of trouble Zoe could cause him and stayed far away.

Zoe did abruptly leave the farm one day, and I was there to see it happen. It was just a few days after I started back to work my last summer. Lenny finished high school the year before and had been working on the farm full-time ever since. Zoe was my age, and we had just graduated. This would be my last summer here before I started college in the fall, and Zoe was making big plans of her own.

After two and a half days of hectic field work, Lenny and I finally had a few minutes to catch up and were sitting in the barn office. The same space that we cleaned out and were prepping for this remodel a couple of years earlier. The same place where our enmity ended and a great friendship was born. Where a few days later, Lenny gave his sins and his heart to Jesus.

He was showing me the plans he and his dad had created to expand the milking parlor in a year or two. Lenny had drawn them himself. I was impressed and telling him so when we heard and saw an old white pickup truck with a few rusty dings and a "customized" V-shaped rear bumper and tailgate come into the barn yard. "Oh yeah," I thought, as I remembered hearing something about a truck that backed into the outside corner of the high school gym just a few weeks ago.

Naturally, we dropped what we were doing and kept an eye on the truck, expecting to have to take care of some kind of business or other. But the driver was looking around nervously, like he didn't know what he was looking for. He was a young guy, or at least he seemed to be. Maybe it was just his small stature compared to the loud, oversized truck that made him appear so young.

We were watching out the window as the driver, swiveling his head back and forth, drove slowly around the circle when we heard a loud whistle.

The truck stopped suddenly, and Zoe stepped out of the tool shed carrying a bright red suitcase, a laundry bag that looked like it was full of shoes, and a bunch of long coats draped over one shoulder. She threw the coats and the bag in the truck's bed and then tried to swing the suitcase over the side, but it was too high. Zoe was trying again when the driver killed the engine and opened his door like he was coming to help her. Zoe shouted out, "Don't be stupid, Vic! Stay in there and be ready to go! I got this without you!" And she got under the suitcase enough to heave it up and over. Then she rushed for the passenger door, which was stuck, and she swore at it and at Victor, whom I suddenly recognized as a guy from our senior class. I saw Victor reach way over, disappearing behind the bench seat from our angle of view, and the passenger door popped open. He was saying something we couldn't hear, but I heard Zoe shout, "Big deal! Congratulations, my hero! Let's go already!"

Lenny and I hadn't moved a muscle and just peered out the glass as the engine came back to life with a roar, and the truck spun around the far curve and took off back up the long driveway. Then we looked at each other and shook our heads. "Looks like Zoe's going to Goodwill to donate all of her clothes," Lenny suggested. "Could be. I only hope she remembers to keep that waitress uniform she was wearing. I have a feeling she might need that for a long time," I said semi-prophetically. "Did I see the 'Drakes' logo on her top?" That's when Lenny filled me in with the latest family news.

It seems that Zoe realized the whining and excuse-making were not working on her dad anymore, so rather than be forced to start doing actual barn work for the first time, Zoe took a job waitressing at Drakes. Then she manipulated Victor Legend into renting a room with her in town. "Just you and me," she told him. "Let's live together where the air don't smell like cow crap all the time!" Zoe was excited because even though her new job was already a "real *cash* cow," it would be "just a first step" on the way to her real career, she said. And Victor thought he had won the jackpot when she started coming back to their place with leftover french fries every night!

"She's been here ever since," I thought dismally. "So many missteps." And just then, I happened to see Zoe trip over her own foot as she was stepping away from the cash register. She caught herself immediately—she always has—and nobody else even noticed the stumble, but once again, I found myself playing the part of the quasi-prophet regarding Zoe; "Eventually she would go down and not recover."

With that thought, came my answer to Zoe's question. I continued going into Drakes periodically, for years at that point, to foster my own "recovery." Zoe was there still working to escape from the farm life she inherently despised, for no good reason. For her, Drakes was some kind of refuge, and my visits intruded on her sanctuary.

In my case, Drakes had become more like a touchpoint, a physical place where I could "make contact," as it were, with both the highest highlights and the meanest sorrowful darkness forever attached to my relationship with Teddy. We had the most wonderful conversation that evening! Full of our usual fun and flirting, and it was made doubly poignant by the fact that I had so stupidly offended her earlier that evening, only to have her pour her love and forgiveness over me! No, we did not enjoy a meal that last night, but we were eagerly heading home to physically express to each other the great love we so thoroughly enjoyed all day and every day.

Even though the doorway at Drakes had been replaced entirely, I still found that location to be the nexus of our love. Teddy gave her life up for me there, again, this time physically and totally, in the ultimate way. Not deliberately, of course. She did not throw herself in front of me to take that shot, knowingly sacrificing her life to save mine. But I know in my knower that she would have willingly done so.

Perhaps it was time for me to consider letting Zoe have her refuge. And for me to internalize my heart's connection to Teddy instead of relying on that piece of real estate. After all, I know that I will see Teddy again, and all of life's turbulence will disappear like mist.

Without the Lord in her life, Zoe would continue to need whatever crutch she could find.

CHAPTER 10

THE MEDITATIONS

"I guess I put it off long enough," I told myself while pushing the pie plate away. I'd had to ask another waitress if I could get a slice of cherry pie because Zoe had carefully avoided the "Epaphras zone" for well over an hour. The pie was good, but I was glad I had broken off the wide, dry end of the crust and eaten that first. I always liked my last bite of pie to be full of the actual pie flavoring it was named for.

Then I had to laugh at myself as I admitted that I was continually distracting myself from getting to Charles's mysterious note.

I pulled the envelope out of my pocket and laid it on the table. "What is wrong with me? I was so eager to read it yesterday when I couldn't, but as soon as I could, I didn't!" I reminded myself of Paul the apostle when he said, "I don't understand what I do. What I want to do I do not do, but what I hate I do." I could relate. He went on to say, "I have the desire to do what is good, but I cannot carry it out. For I do not do the good I want to do, but the evil I do not want to do—this I keep on doing!"

"*Ha!*" I said, and even out loud! A few people looked over at me. I blushed, but not just because of the attention. But because I was using *Scripture* to distract myself from doing what I should be doing! "I bet that not even Paul, the 'chief of sinners,' could ever say that!"

There was an apparently leftover Fourth of July greeting card in the prison, made just of copy paper, in the envelope. More of a prison-related gag card, really. On the front, it said, "Happy Freedom Day," and on the inside, it said, "From your friends in the *big house!*" I had to unfold the paper card completely before I found a very brief, very shocking, handwritten note on the inside.

It said, "Epifras, Not sure I can handel this Big job as plannd. But can we keep on so I Can keep being out of my cell? Happy Forth!"

I looked over the envelope inside and out and turned the paper over very carefully a few times to see if there was anything that would tell me this was just a bad joke. Nothing there.

I was confused and baffled and dumbstruck. I had thought Charles was at least a potential writer, but why did I think that? I guess I thought…or rather, assumed…

"What's that? Fourth of July was like ten days ago!" Zoe charged as she slid into "her" chair across the table. She had snuck up on me again, and I almost jumped out of my chair, at least from the waist up, at the sound of her abrasive voice! "Zoe! Do you always assail your customers like that? Geez!" I said as I grabbed the paper and hastily stuffed it back in my "man pocket" in the form of a wadded ball. As she sat there with a big, satisfied smile, I realized my complaints would only encourage her and determined to avoid giving her any footing.

"Queenie told me to get you anything you want. And free of charge, so I am checking to see what else you might want." And then felt the need to add: "And I mean from the menu," she said, winking. No, neither of her eyelids even twitched, but I felt an intentional, toying wink directed at me. "Maybe a nice hot cup of coffee?" she said, knowing already for many years that I did not drink coffee. "Isn't it time you start acting like an adult?" Maybe it was just me, but it seems that Zoe's use of double entendres was only barely hidden.

One of the things Lenny used to harass me about back on the farm was my straightforward aversion to coffee. But Zoe, back on the farm, thought it was cute and used to come to my defense. "He doesn't want to become an addic' like you are!" she taunted Lenny, even though she drank at least as much, and at a younger age, as he did. That was before Zoe realized that I would end up being more closely allied with Lenny than with her. When Lenny cut his coffee intake way back and to the point where even now he only has an occasional cup, coffee became symbolic of the new division.

"No, thank you, Zoe," I said dismissively, and then asked with more sincerity than I thought possible, "Is there anything I can do for you? How have you been?"

She saw immediately that I was not going to take the bait on the coffee thing, and certainly not any other thing, and that we would not be arguing about that today. My guileless questions seemed to strike her like a slap, and she suddenly jumped up like she was at work or something and had customers to wait on and said, "I am perfectly fine! Better than you'll ever be. And dandy too!" She took off in the direction of the back door before stopping short and turning around to head instead back toward the kitchen. An older man sitting with his wife smiled up at Zoe and waved a hopeful hand toward her as she went by, but she did not stop or even acknowledge him. I heard his wife raise her voice to him for not stopping her, and then he threw up his hands and pointed angrily at me!

If only to avoid eye contact with him, I looked at my watch and then began to wonder where Barnabas was. And Queenie. Someone more responsible and saner than Zoe needs to be running this operation.

"What a day!" and my hand went to the lump in my coat. "Charles, oh brother!" I thought, with a disgusted grunt. And then, "Greg! And Charles! And Barnabas. And Zoe!" I whined, considering my recent troublemakers, whether frustrating and confusing like Greg and Charles, merely distracted and annoying like Barn today, or downright scary and threatening like Zoe. And then, of course, I thought about my Teddy. I missed her comfort and her wisdom.

"Oh, but Charles, what am I going to do about

you?" I knew already that one way or another, I would continue to go see Charles. After all, I went to the prison and met him for the first time without any thoughts about having my story written. It was ministry then, and would be back to "mere" ministry again. "But what am I going to say to him?" I asked myself. "And how did I let myself get into this whole thing anyway? I let Charles convince me that he could write a great story and get it published, based on what? Just his own claims! And why? Because of my own ego," I had to admit! "Oh Lord, forgive me!"

I also knew I would have to go see the warden to keep things above board with him. How would he react? Would he still let us meet in the conference room once he knew it was all a charade? Or would our visits revert back to the actual visitor's room, where we would be separated by the glass divider? "Charles!" I said, this time right out loud, and began to think about how a simple jail ministry had turned into this research and interview project. About a minute later, my thoughts were interrupted when the dishwasher again appeared at my table, this time with dripping hands! "Yes, sir?" He looked at me, "I'm Charley." "Hi, Charley," I said and just looked at him expectantly. "Can I do something for you? Your waitress Zoe said you called for me. Did you have a dirty glass or something?" As I looked up, I saw the door to the kitchen swing shut and heard Zoe's classic "gotcha" laughter ring out inside. "Oh, no, thank you. Everything is perfectly clean, Charles. Zoe misunderstood something, I guess. I apologize for the inconvenience. But you are doing a great job!" As he strode back to his sink, looking confused and angry, I almost yelled out "Zoe!" very loudly, but I was learning to control myself a little, so instead, I only rolled my eyes… but quite adamantly!

After some years of working together in the men's ministry at church, Yeti and I finally decided to go try prison ministry. So early in the fall of 2011, we went through the application process and were authorized as prison chaplains. It was just a designation that allowed us to visit non-related inmates. Like one of those superficial "ordinations" a person can get online so they can then "marry" their friends. Then we contacted the state prison at Riverside and made ourselves available and were surprised to hear back in less than two weeks. Wardens understand that prisoners need visitors, so they take all they can get.

We were given a list of twenty-five prisoners who had requested Christian ministry visits and immediately got letters out to all of them. By the

EPAPHRAS: THE INTERVIEW

middle of February, there we were, Yeti and I, sitting in the visiting center waiting to be paired up with whoever followed through that day to talk to the "preacher boys."

Yeti was nervous at first. He told me that his first thought as we went through the maze of security was, "What if?" How close had he come to making that one big mistake or rash decision that could have put him on the "visitee" side of the wall? I agreed with him. Any one of us sinners could have ended up, and still can end up, in serious trouble. Yeti and I both had the "there but for the grace of God go I" thought run through our minds while we waited.

Another thing we had in common was that our exposure to rough talk and rough treatment may have prepared us for this time. Yeti had to put up with his father, and then with himself, for years! I had to deal intensely with Lenny and then Yeti, too (Sorry, big guy!), for some time, so we both had relatively thick skin.

Yeti, however, discovered that his own loud-mouth, belligerent past life prepared him well for dealing with the abusive jokes and antagonistic attitude first presented by his new "friends" in prison. He didn't flinch when the first guy he met took one look and called him Sasquatch even though his name tag said Rick (using our own nicknames was discouraged by the prison staff). Yeti simply took that as an opening, however. He smiled and said, "Not Sasquatch. Call me Yeti." The guy laughed and called him Bigfoot! Yeti, I mean Rick, laughed at that twist, and the ice was broken.

The inmates were very quick and creative to come up with great monikers for us. There were the obvious ones. They called me "Crips" or "The Chairman" or "David" (when I was seen with Yeti, who was quickly identified as "Goliath"). I also heard "Stevie" (as in Steven Hawkins), "Wheely," and "Daisy Mae" (Dais ye see me Rollin'?).

But after I met maybe four or five different inmates, one guy took a good look at me as I was sitting in my wheelchair, trying to look like somebody with something to offer. I smiled at him and, throwing caution to the wind in an effort to create trust right away, gave him the man's universal positive head nod (chin moving upward first like a man does when he encounters someone he knows instead of downward first when merely acknowledging a stranger on the sidewalk). He returned the favor, giving me the upward nod with his noticeably large head and a smile. Then he looked at me seriously. And showed me that he was one of those rare "nicknamers" who really had the gift. Not just knowing how to turn a phrase but showing a deeper power of discernment or sensitivity to another man's nature or condition.

"I'm gonna call you 'Woebe,'" he said. His name was Charles, but I eventually came to call him "Chuck."

"Why 'Woebe'?" I asked hesitantly. I think I knew what was coming.

"Woebegone," he said, "which does not mean that all your woes be gone as you might expect. It's the opposite. It means buried with woe. You seem sad to me," he said sympathetically, "even with the smile. And not just 'cause of the chair. Is that a permanent thing?"

I was surprised by the clever wordsmithing this Charles guy had come up with so easily, and my face must have shown it because he looked at me, and before I could get to answering his question, he said, "I do a lot of puzzle books. Especially the ones with word games. Is it permanent?"

"Do you mean the smile or the chair? Or...the sad?" I asked. Then without waiting for an answer and deciding that this guy deserves full disclosure, I went on to answer all three parts. "The chair I've had for a long time and expect to for the rest of my life. The smile stems from the joy of the Lord in my heart, so it too is permanent."

"What about the sad part? I actually meant the sad," Charles said.

"Well. I didn't expect to go into that today, but you really showed me that you are a very insightful person. Besides, I have a little folder here that tells me a few things about your background, so I guess it's only fair for you to know a little more about me."

"Oh yeah? What do they tell you about me in there?"

I was glad to let the subject change. "Not much, really," I said, opening the small file. "Looks like you just turned thirty years old…on New Year's Day? That's cool!" I said.

"Meh," Charles answered, "people used to always remember my birthday, which was cool, but it was always at the last minute and with a hangover. What else?"

"I suppose. It says you're from my area. Did you grow up in Chase? We moved there when I was five." No answer but a slight shrug. I went on. "It looks like you only have another year and a half to go in here. Six years for aggravated assault. That seems like a harsh sentence. Do you want to talk about that?" I was open to talking about my "sad," as he had called it, but I thought it would be good to get on with the ministry part of this "ministry visit" too. The part where I would minister to *him*, that is!

"No. Not really," he said, looking at the floor. I was about to go on with my story when Charles quietly added, "I got off easy." And then he jumped up like he was anxious to get back to me being the subject and asked, "Well? Why are you so sad? Why so woebegone, Woebe? You've been in that chair for twelve years, you say, and you're still not over it?"

It wasn't my favorite of all the nicknames I've been given, but he didn't even seem to notice that my real name was so vulnerable to attack, so I played along with a chuckle and said, "Yeah, about that. I'm not really sad about the legs, at least not anymore. You see, Charles, I caught a bullet in the spine one night that paralyzed me from the waist down. But the same bullet first went through my beautiful young wife. It killed her outright and then cut me down good at the same time. I was right behind her." Still no answer. Not even a "Wow!"

"If I'm sad," I went on slowly, "it's because I loved her so much, and I miss her so much. She loved me too, and I miss that. So yes, I do have a regular burden of 'sad' over my life that not everyone can recognize without already knowing the story. But you did." He looked at me, acknowledging his gift, and then looked past me at the wall as if he was trying to form a disconnect that would stop my sadness from transferring over to him.

"I'm okay without the legs working, and I have the solid hope of seeing Teddy again in heaven. Because Jesus died to save us both, and both of us repented of our sins and are redeemed, I know that she is in heaven waiting for me and that one day I will be there with Jesus and Teddy *and* with two working legs too!" "There!" I thought. "A little bit of ministry by way of testimony!"

And then I braced for the usual barrage of questions. It would start with "Who did it?" and then go to either "Why were you two shot?" or "Where did it happen?" and, of course, "Did they catch the shooter?" This was always difficult for me because I had no good answers. "I still don't know who did it or why. The only thing I do know is that it happened at a restaurant in Chase. No, they never caught anybody. They never even had a suspect." I rehearsed in my mind, just to be ready to get past this part quickly.

But he didn't ask. Hopefully, Charles was considering the last bit I said about Jesus and heaven and Teddy. But he just continued staring at the wall. His reaction confirmed my impression that Charles was some kind of an "empath." "Like Deanna Troi," I told myself, "He isn't asking those questions because he already 'feels' the important answers and doesn't care about the mundane facts of my personal tragedy." I was greatly relieved to find that I did not have to try—only to fail—to answer the basic questions I always heard. And even better, I did not have to answer why I did not know the answers!

But Charles did surprise me with one more bomb. "What about your 'mad'?" he queried.

"I'm not mad at all," I said, quibbling and probably turning red. And I wanted to punch him!

"You're not mad?" and looked deeply at me, and it seemed he was checking his antennae to correct for a problem with the reception. "Why not? I pushed a lady off a bench at a bus stop, and she made sure I went to jail for a year over a bruised butt! Some guy shoots you and your wife outside a restaurant, and you're not hot in the collar? I don't believe it. Tell me about your mad, and maybe sometime we'll talk about my assaults and stuff."

I really was not prepared for all of this! I don't know what I expected today, but it wasn't some lame prisoner challenging the most tender parts of my heart and soul.

I wanted to keep up with the denial. I tried, but my tongue got all tied up, and I couldn't. "A curst... uh-corse...yeah, I'd been angry...in past...in the past I was," I said clumsily. I realized that I was gripping the hand rims on the wheels of my chair so tightly that my hands were going numb. As I got hold of myself, I let go of the wheels. Charles waited patiently and did not say a word while I massaged both of my palms in turn and gathered my strength.

Then, deliberately, I broke down and admitted the truth with an easy calm. "Of course, I'm angry, Chuck. May I call you Chuck?" He gave one silent nod. "Still angry as the day I woke up in the hospital without working legs and then found out that some fool had killed, taken, my wife. A terrible wrong was done, and I hate the fact of it. I want justice to come to...somebody. I don't know if it's to me or for Teddy or down on the perpetrator, but I do want to see justice."

I took the hand rims in hand again and rocked the chair back and forth while I thought about it.

"Charles had somehow broken into my heart, and a portion of that famed river in Egypt began to leak out," I told myself. As the denial receded, I could suddenly confess what I had been suppressing for a long time. The anger, justified but kept under wraps, was there, and instead of fighting it, I was at first greatly relieved to concede its existence. Then I had to reconcile anger with love.

God's people are told, "Clothe yourselves with compassion, kindness, humility, gentleness, and patience." And I had. But I was still wearing and justifying the dirty long johns of my own anger underneath! I was in a quandary, hovering somewhere between holding on to my sinful humanity and giving myself wholly over to God's perfect model. Yes, I serve a just God who will one day make all things right. But I also know that He loves mercy as much as He loves justice. So more than intently craving some form of justice for Teddy's murder, I want to be like God and practice forgiveness. "Lord, help me," I prayed silently.

As I pondered my way to that last short prayer, the silence grew thick between us. I don't know what he was thinking, but I was tempted to tell him way more than he could handle just then.

"But there is so much more to it, Charles, that I doubt you can understand." He looked me in the eye and seemed a little shaken. I imagine he did not really expect me to both admit the anger like that and keep it under control in the end. "Oh, maybe you can. You have some kind of a gift of discernment going for you. I have a friend with a similar gift. We call him X-Ray. But if you haven't heard the gospel and accepted it, I am not so sure you can understand the whole of what I believe and feel inside."

He hesitated, but then Charles gave way to another insistent impulse and said, "Try me."

I let out a long stream of air, so glad to see how God had directed this whole conversation. He had used Charles to break through my pride so I could admit what I thought should have been hidden, both for my sake and for His! I slowly spun my chair in a circle and offered a great big smile to the Lord before coming back around to face Chuck with a ministerially straight face. I believe that the Lord reminded me during that traverse of some very appropriate verses for me to share just then.

"We are just about out of time, sir," I said, "but let me tell you about a couple of Bible verses that apply to our discussion. First of all, anger is quite

EPAPHRAS: THE INTERVIEW

often an appropriate response to troubles. Especially to troubles caused by sin... like murder! God gets angry at sin, for sure, but He handles it perfectly. And He tells us, first in Psalm 4:4, and then quoted in the book of Ephesians 6 in the New International Version of the Bible, 'In your anger do not sin.' And it goes on to say, 'Do not let the sun go down while you are still angry!' In other words, anger has its place, but don't let it lead you down a sour and hurtful path! I guess I was kind of harboring my anger, protecting it from being diffused, maybe hoping to unleash it one day on the perp if he is ever caught. Wow. And I didn't even know it, Chuck! Thank you for asking me about the 'mad' that you somehow perceived in me! I feel much better now."

I was about to go on, not expecting an answer from Charles, when he said, "You are welcome, I guess, but now I can tell you that I was really just messing with you, trying to keep you talking about anything but me by pretending I was some kind of *Star Trek* counselor or something, I don't know."

"Ha!" I laughed, especially at the inside knowledge that we were both Trekkies, and said, "Okay, but I think God used it all for good, for both of us! Maybe now the killer can be identified because God won't have to worry about me playing the vigilante or executioner! He's got this under control, and He wants me to be more forgiving than angry."

"And the thing is, now, Epps—you may have heard that nickname before—now I do want to hear what you have to say about all of this stuff! Did you say that a *couple* of verses came to mind? Did you say them already?"

I was shocked and in awe of God. I told Him so, mentally, and then remembered the other verse I wanted to share with Chuck. "There is another one. It's in Colossians 3," I said. "This verse is the one that has truly guided my life since the murder, though apparently, I've been keeping some measure of sinful anger hidden from its attention. Sorry to say.

"I want you to know about it because it expresses not only how I should feel about the…perpetrator, in my case, but this is how the victims you assaulted should proceed in their dealings with you. If they want to obey God and do what is right, that is. Now, Chuck, I want you to know I am not making this stuff up! So write this down so you can check on me as soon as you can. The Bible verse I want to share with you is from Colossians 3:13. In the NIV translation, it says, 'Bear with each other and forgive *whatever* grievances you may have against one another. *Forgive as the Lord forgave you.*' The emphasis is on the word 'whatever'! Which certainly includes being pushed off a bench, right?"

Charles smiled broadly at that idea and was taken by surprise when the door suddenly opened, and a guard walked in to collect his prisoner and return him to his cell. Charles shouldn't have been too shocked, but he looked at the guard and at his watch like he had been abruptly and recklessly shaken awake from the best part of a great dream.

He got to his feet right away when told to but tried to put the guard off for a minute while he launched into one more high-speed question for me. The guard was methodical and gave him no slack. When Charles did not start walking toward the door, he was taken by the elbow, and a second guard was called.

"Is your story in print anywhere, Woebe?" he asked in the commotion, almost pleading. "It's quite the drama. Here you are, in a wheelchair, sad and lonely, and a little mad, but out visiting state convicts!" as he went through the doorway under pressure. Before the door closed all the way, I heard him yelling out: "I think this story should be told! I just met you, and I can think of a thousand questions that should be answered!" And after the door was fully closed, I thought I heard Charles' desperate voice yelling, "I'll write the story myself!"

Too stunned by having just witnessed so much real-life state-prison drama so close at hand, I did not register exactly what Charles was yelling about until Yeti and I were en route back to Chase. First, I asked Yeti about his encounters that day. This was our first time working in the prison ministry, so we started out with a lot of questions, fears, and hopes. Now, on the way home, we had a few answers, even more questions to ask, and a mixed bag of fears either overcome or exacerbated and hopes either realized or shot down. It was complicated because people—including ourselves—are complicated, and we were both glad to have a long drive back to debrief.

Once again, Yeti expressed how grateful to God he was for delivering him from his sins! He was certain that without the Lord intervening, the path he had been on was heading right to this jail. I joined with him in praising God. But I also gave him credit for the right decisions he had made, which truly allowed the Lord to do that good work in his life.

Then I told Yeti about my afternoon. He was amazed by the way this Charles guy had seen right into me, and he was excited to hear about the testimony and the verses I was able to share. And then I pieced together for him and myself what Chuck had been yelling about when he was being "escorted" back to his cell. "Crazy, huh?" I said. "Writing something about *me*?"

But Rick really surprised me by saying, "What? No! You haven't thought of that? I guess I wouldn't have expected some convict to suggest it, but yes, Epps, your story needs to be out there for sure." Then he shocked me by adding, "The guys have been saying that for years!"

As I was still sitting at Drakes, not *deliberately* taking full advantage of Queenie's generous blank-check offer but fully enjoying a bowl of broccoli cheddar soup and some onion rings nonetheless, I remembered that I had been rather dismayed by Charles' idea and Rick's unbridled enthusiasm over it. He had told me, "The guys have been saying that for years!" "Well, no one ever floated it by me!" I thought, with just a little bit of rancor. Maybe it was that news and that feeling that goaded me into jumping in so quickly when the opportunity arose. "Maybe I do deserve a little credit," was the prideful thought that led to the current and inevitable point of deflation.

"And Teddy deserves a ton of credit!" I quickly added, as if I was afraid she was reading my thoughts and would have felt left out. There had been local news stories right after the shooting, but nothing more than that. "So much came out of this tragedy over the years, too, and yes, my Teddy should be known and remembered…forever!" I thought.

And the rest is history. Or it might have been. Then I found out that Charles couldn't even spell a few basic words and that he was probably scamming me all along just to get a little more time free of his prison cell. "Right now," my angry flesh was telling me, "that is precisely where he deserves to be!"

I closed my eyes, not to humble myself before God, not to confess that my pride and visions of grandeur were gaining control of me, but as I savored the last mouthful of soup, swirling it around in my mouth to collect all of its varied flavors, I was similarly relishing the sympathies, the acclaim, and even the royalties that might have come pouring in when my story went straight to the top of the bestseller list. "Oh brother," I said aloud, shaking my head and opening my eyes, just as Barnabas and Queenie were trying to secretly slide into the seats across from me!

"Busted!" Barnabas said disappointedly when I saw them, and he and Queenie both laughed giddily over their attempt and gave me credit for supposedly detecting and downplaying their game.

"Oh brother!" I said again with a smile. This time, pretending to mock them for playing such a childish game. They knew I was enjoying it, but they did not know that I was also feeling grateful to be roused from my self-gratifying, self-glorifying, self-deceiving meditations.

"Barn!" I interjected, "Can you take me over to Riverside on Monday?"

"Sure thing, but don't you mean Tuesday? Tuesday, Thursday, and Friday, I thought."

"Monday. I need to see the warden. Then we'll know about the other days."

CHAPTER 11

THE ASSAULT

Poor Krispy. After Queenie and Barny told me about their afternoon together—and profusely apologized for being gone for almost *four* hours—they stepped over behind the front desk to say goodbye while I pushed myself toward the door to wait. I didn't mean to intrude, but I saw Barnabas give Queenie a quick kiss on the cheek. She smiled sweetly, looked up at him with appreciation, and said, "Can I give you a hug?" Barn readily consented, and I looked away. As I turned, I caught a glimpse of Zoe watching from where she was standing next to a crowded table with her pad in hand and busily ignoring the customers trying to give their orders. She watched the interaction, and I could see plainly that she was not happy about it. "Oh, brother," I said once again, but this time to myself. Barn finally let go of Queenie, and I heard him say "Goodbye," and

EPAPHRAS: THE INTERVIEW

then, "I'll ask later," and floated dreamily over to me with a silly puppy-dog look on his face, and I finally got to go home!

When Sunday morning came, I was very happy to be in church! To hear the teaching of God's Word and to worship Him along with my fellow believers! Especially after the long Saturday I spent alone at Drakes. There, I sat in my chair all day while one burden after another was set on my shoulders. Then on Sunday, I was able to sit, again, in my chair, in the back of the sanctuary where one pew had been removed to make room for the wheelchair-bound, but instead of being weighed down with more problems, I got to "cast all of my burdens on Jesus! Because He cares for me."

I was anxious to begin praying about the "burdens" in my life, but the effort was interrupted and delayed as several good friends passing by my "pew" stopped to offer handshakes, smiles, and blessings. In their own way, these greetings each began to relieve my load. Then, once the service began, I brought my list of concerns to the Lord, "wrestling," as it were, and praying with hope and thanksgiving.

I started with Zoe. "Lord, would You help Zoe? I've known her a long time and still can't understand how to approach her. I know she needs You, but she resists so strenuously. Please soften her heart, deliver her from trouble, and bring her to Yourself. Thank You for the way You've used Zoe to challenge my walk with You."

And I prayed for Charles. "Again, Lord, I don't know what to do about Charles. What is the best answer? Help me to know what to do. I forgive him for seemingly setting me up and for dropping the ball. Help me to reach him with Your love and salvation." And for Barnabas. "Thank You for Barny. I love him like a son—though I was only eleven when he was born—but You know what I mean. Please do bless his life by meeting his needs and answering his many fervent prayers."

And I went on to pray for Queenie in the same vein, and for her parents, for the other guys currently involved in the men's group, like poor/perfect Ned, X-Ray, Krispy, Wade, Victor (!), and Isaac, and all of their families, and then, all of a sudden, I found myself praying for Greg!

Probably, because, at one point that morning, I had looked up and saw him eyeing me from across the sanctuary! When I looked a few minutes later, he was watching me again. It wasn't one of those

EPAPHRAS: THE INTERVIEW

casual glances like he had turned to see the clock or something, but it seemed more like a twist-around-in-your-seat and get-a-crick-in-the-neck kind of surveillance, which was fitting since Greg had long been a pain in my neck. Was this his best-practices method of apologizing to me for yesterday?

"Sorry, Lord, but I don't know what to think about Greg. He confuses me and makes me mad and even a little scared lately, but You know what he needs. You know. Please help him, and yes, use me if You can. I am willing."

They say, "The only problem with working with people is the people." I will testify that "they" were right! Back in 2001, with about two years of chair living under my belt, I got the church's approval to organize a men's group and started meeting with a small group of about five guys every other Saturday. I learned to love them all dearly, especially over time, but just like me, everyone carries an issue or two that need addressing, and I made it my business to help with that addressing. It was always fulfilling ministry, but it was always a challenge too.

Arty and Oscar, the two old coots, were like anchors for me. My childhood friend X-Ray, Ray Harris, was always interesting to work with and to watch in action, but he always kept me on my toes too! And there was Rick, whom I still thought of as Yeti! He could be somewhat impetuous and volatile, as I can testify after working with him in construction, but as he came to welcome the Lord deeper and deeper into his heart, we both discovered a very tender and kind side growing underneath. It was beautiful to see! And to top off the original regulars at our group, young Barnabas, who joined us late in the first year when he was just seventeen, came in with his own set of custom baggage to unpack along with remarkable gifts to be discovered.

But Greg.

"But Greg?" my new interviewer said.

"Yes. Let me set this up for you. After graduating, in '97, Teddy and I were married and moved to Chase, as you know. Amazingly, we had both landed jobs at the elementary school and started teaching that fall. We had a wonderful but short honeymoon and then spent some hectic weeks moving into our new home in Chase and preparing our classrooms! I still can't believe we put ourselves through all of that so fast!

"Anyway, I later remembered seeing Greg at church every once in a while, but I never talked to him.

EPAPHRAS: THE INTERVIEW

In fact, when I saw him at Drakes the night of the shooting, I did not recognize him. I think that was partly because of his disgusting behavior that night. I was not inclined to associate him with church.

"But here he was in 2012, a regular, if still under suspicion, MG attendee and a regular at church. And then, all of a sudden, guilty of assaulting a cripple in a wheelchair and of staring at an invalid through a whole church service!"

"Oh my," she deadpanned.

Ignoring the affront barely hidden in that remark, I offered instead a flashback to 2003. "The men's group was really picking up; after averaging about five guys per meeting through the first year, we were up to twenty or twenty-five in the spring of '03! So, one Sunday before Easter, Greg walked into church, and I thought I should do the right thing, so I rolled over and started talking to him and ended up inviting him to the men's group meeting, explaining that we called it MG and we get together about every other Saturday morning. I warned him that we meet at 6 a.m., but he was all excited to be there anyway. 'Of course, I am an avid morning person!' he said, seemingly hurt that I did not make that presumption.

"We talked a little more, or at least he did, waxing

eloquent about the benefits of exercising vigorous morning habits and the beautiful stringency of his daily disciplines in general. While he was talking, I suddenly heard, from behind me, X-Ray say very loudly to Barnabas, who was passing by, 'Hey, Barnabas, did we have our men's group meeting last week or yesterday? I forgot.' And then I heard Barn answer, 'What? If it was yesterday, don't you think you'd remember that?' 'Well, you know me. I have a memory like a steel sieve,' X answered, and I knew something was up because that guy still remembers getting his diaper changed! 'But when is the next meeting?' he asked Barnabas, who answered quite loudly while he was walking away, 'Next Saturday, the nineteenth. At six in the morning, in case you forgot that too!'

"Greg stiffened and looked confused for a second before stretching himself up to full height in order to better look down at me with scorn and said, 'Excuse me, Mr. Mallas, do I understand that your men's group is meeting *next* Saturday?' 'Yes, that's right. The last one was last weekend, so…' 'On *Holy* Saturday?' he challenged combatively. 'What's that?' I asked honestly but thought to myself, 'Isn't *every* Saturday holy?' 'Holy Saturday,' he said most seriously, 'is the day between Good Friday and

Resurrection Sunday. It is known as "The Day of Waiting at the Tomb," and in some higher circles, it is considered a most solemn time. It should be spent fasting and in vigilance, not laughing and eating donuts and rehearsing each other's moral failures.' He looked at me like he was waiting for applause. Or at least an announcement that the MG meeting would be rescheduled and maybe for me to call out for repentance in sackcloth and ashes.

"With that failing, he went on to inform me that, regretfully, he could not attend on such an important day. I was assuring him that I understood and that he would certainly be welcome any other Saturday that worked for him, etc., etc. when I heard a low 'Huh' coming from over my shoulder. I turned in my chair and saw X-Ray, who had been standing behind me, now striding away up the aisle biting on a Styrofoam cup! By the time I turned back around, Greg was gone, and I started to think I was surrounded by kooks!

"Now I know that Greg (who was sometimes called 'Gregor' as in Gregor Mendel, the father of genetics, by some of the wise guys in our group because he was considered to be something of a 'seedy' character) was no kook. And neither was X. They were just two... interesting variations on the theme of fallen man.

"So that was in 2003. Nine years have passed, and I maybe saw Greg nine times in all those years. I think two of those times were at MG. He appeared in church quite randomly. It wasn't just a 'Christmas and Easter' thing like it is for some folks, so I was always surprised when I saw him.

"But that all changed early in 2012. Suddenly, he was in church, alone, every week. Everyone noticed and wondered what was going on. And at the same time, he started coming to the MG meetings every time we had one. In fact, shock of shocks, the first time he walked in was April 7!"

"So?" Macy asked.

"It was *Holy Saturday*! X and I looked at each other with our mouths hanging open as he came in at 5:59 a.m., unshaven, looking like he just dragged himself out of bed, wearing something he had maybe pulled from the laundry pile, and sat down in the back. I didn't make a scene, but I wanted to go take his temperature to find out if he was sick or dying. Even X-Ray was stymied.

"Well, I guess he wasn't really sick or anything. But after that first shock of a visit, Greg kept coming, always just about late and always stubbly and poorly dressed, until that last time, two days ago, that I told you about when he came in early, tidy and ready for the day, and for all practical purposes, nearly accosted me in my chair!"

"Did you use enough qualifiers there, Epps? Did he 'accost' you or not? And you called it 'assault' earlier."

"You know me too well. I can't get away with anything here."

"Well? Did he even come close to 'assaulting' or 'accosting' you?"

"He touched my chair and leaned in close. And… he had ugly nose hair."

"Oh no!"

"*And* he…spoke…uncharitably…about our Teddy."

"Yes. That was on the fourteenth, right?"

"Yes."

"Well. What happened next?"

"Well, nothing much happened the rest of Sunday. Fortunately, I had that easy Sunday afternoon because Monday was rough!

CHAPTER 12

THE INTERVIEW

"On Monday morning, I got to ride in the back seat of my own car for two and a half hours. It wasn't so bad, comfort-wise, but I missed the quiet ride with just me and Barnabas. Typically, he would be praying quietly most of the time, and we would have short, intermittent conversations along the way."

"So…? Why were you in the back seat?"

"I made the mistake of asking Barnabas to drive me over to Riverside in front of Queenie!"

"Oh, I see!"

"Yeah! I noticed her slump a little when he quickly agreed to take me, but I only found out why later on. I guess that when Barn and Queenie were out on their jaunt, she told him that she had Monday off if he wanted to do something. Is that how 'dates' are arranged now, by the way? Anyway, at the time, he wasn't sure if I needed him, so they were pretty hopeful until I asked him to drive me to the prison. But before we left Drakes on Saturday, Queenie asked Barnabas to ask me if she could come along for the ride and keep him company while he waited for me. He asked me later on the way home, and of course I agreed and, on Monday morning, offered to let them sit together in front."

"Okay, but didn't you say something earlier about Kris also liking Queenie?"

"Ah yes, unlike me, you don't miss a thing!" I admitted. "I never thought about that until we were pulling into the parking lot, and I wondered if Barn and Kris would get to say hi again. Then it hit me that Queenie would be right there in the middle, and I wondered if Barn and Kris would kill me together or if they would do it one at a time. And I wondered if Queenie knew that Kris worked there or even that he liked her or if she might like him. I felt like I was back in middle school for a minute! But I'll get back to that later.

"I will say this much now. You know my life has always been full, right? I like to be busy, whether it be at school or work or church; I need to be productive to feel right. Even the paraplegia did not change that part of me. But this past week, since the first day of the interview with Charles on Thursday, has been crazy! I've been faced with one quandary or challenge or emotional episode or threat all week!

"So much talking about all the pivotal people and impactful events from the past. Reliving delights and tragedies and rehearsing the dramas and traumas in the lives of so many close friends and family has been grueling, and I am exhausted!"

"I understand, Epaphras. And there's more, isn't there?"

"Yes. Incredible…I still have incredible stuff to tell you."

"I can wait. Why don't you go back to the prison parking lot on Monday the sixteenth? You just arrived there and were worried about Kris and Barn killing you, supposedly.

"Yeah, I wish that the rest of the story were as simple and straightforward as that minor problem at least should have been."

"Yes, dear."

"Hmm. It was a hot July day, so I told—suggested to—Barn that he should drive all the way over to the far side of the lot where there were a lot of shade

EPAPHRAS: THE INTERVIEW

trees they could park under while they waited for me. Truthfully, I was hoping to hide Queenie as far from the entry as possible in case Kris came out at some point. It wasn't too likely that he would, and my meeting shouldn't take too long anyway, but it turned out that I hadn't thought the whole thing through very well.

"Instead of quickly dropping me off by the entry, in full view of the administration offices, he did drive all the way across the lot to park in the shade and planned to push me back, as I expected. But when Barn got my chair out of the back and I was being helped into it, Queenie jumped out of the car, too, saying how good it was to stand up and stretch after the long ride, and Barn invited her to walk over with us and then back with him. Turns out she loves hot weather and sunshine, so she was all in and grabbed his elbow as we got going.

"When we started out, I called in to let them know I was there for my appointment, hoping a guard would come to the door at the same time we did. But the warden had looked out his window at just the right moment and noticed me being 'unloaded' and sent a guard outside right away to receive me. Guess who."

"Oh no."

"Yes. Of course. See what I mean about the way things went all week? So, Krispy stood outside there and watched the three of us slowly ambling over. I saw him right away, but those two were looking at each other and laughing and seeming like a solid couple from way back, so they did not notice Kris until we were right there."

"Hello, Mr. Mallas. The warden is ready to see you. Hi Barnabas. It's Queenie, right? How are you?"

"Queenie is the only one who answered him. 'I am fine, Kris. Of course, it's Queenie! It's not me who is barely recognizable in a fancy new uniform! You look so snazzy!' she said, and Barn looked down at his cutoffs. Kris relaxed and brightened a bit under Queenie's attention. 'Thank you! I appreciate that coming from you!' he said. 'I know you too. I just didn't know you two were a couple,' and he looked ruefully at Barnabas, who had not said anything about Queenie when they talked just last week.

"A *couple*!" she said, with more distaste expressed than felt. "We're just hanging out…" She looked at Barnabas, who looked stricken. "…so far." Then she looked confused. "And only since Saturday!" Barn injected, hoping to get himself off the hook with his friend, which only rumpled Queenie's thoughts all the more.

"And so it went! I was sitting down there in my chair, looking up at the three of them dragging each other into a vortex of hurt and confusion. Round and round they went! Like a three-party game of ping pong where each player tried to knock the balls of insecurity, misgivings, and suspicion away from themselves and toward their friends."

"Finally, I said, 'What time is it, Kris? We better go in?'

"Kris seemed to wake up to the real world around him and said, 'Oh crap!' Then he abruptly stepped between Barnabas and the back of my chair, taking full control of it as if winning that battle could assure his victory over Barnabas in the battle for Queenie's heart! Then we took off for the gate like the bogyman was after us! I did not dare lessen my grip on the chair to wave goodbye to the so recently infatuated but now rankled pair for fear of being rolled out of it onto the sidewalk!"

"Okay, but how did it go with the warden? You tend to get bogged down in details, Epps, and I'm trying to get the whole story here."

"You too? Charles always said the same thing! But

readers like details! I think you shou—"

"Hold on! I only said that I might, maybe, think about writing the story for you. Don't get ahead of yourself again."

"Oh, brother. See what I mean about this week? I can't get a break!"

"I'm not your brother. I'm your sister. Now can you tell me about your talk with the warden, or do I have to hear all about the décor of his office first?"

"Oh, bro… What warden? Oh yeah! The warden! Yeah, that was another treat!"

"First of all, Kris didn't say a—"

"The *warden*!"

"Okay, okay! I showed him the note I got from Charles, crumpled and wrinkly as it was, and explained my dilemma," I offered and almost stopped there as if I didn't really understand where to draw the line between too many and too few details. She didn't bite, so I went on.

"Well, first, he was very curious about the project. He had been previously, too, of course. But now, after listening to, or should I say eavesdropping on, our discussion down in the conference room, he really wanted to know what I expected to come from this so-called 'interview.' Even without seeing the note, the warden said that he had doubted that Charles was ever really interested in writing anything. Partially simply because he had the advantage of seeing Chuck's file and knowing the results of his aptitude tests. There was no indication there that Charles could write a coherent article. Beyond that, the warden knows prisoners in general and knows that they are usually up to something and that they always know how to game the system."

"So why did he ever allow the interview to take place? That's crazy!"

"I know! That's what I said, too, in different words, of course. But I asked him the same question."

"Well?"

"The warden said that he was just so intrigued with this whole thing that he had to find out what it was all about. And with the cameras and the ability to know firsthand what was going on down there, he knew nothing foul could happen. Nothing dangerous, that is. Right about then, though, I noticed that he picked up the crunchy note again and absentmindedly pelletized it. He didn't say so, but I think he was a little embarrassed that we were able to get a note passed between us *and* removed from the prison without his knowing about it.

"He did tell me that he wanted to find out what I might be up to, which was nothing, of course. At least nothing nefarious. Other than my own nefarious ego trip, anyway. Which, to my own shame, I did confess to him, with the attached declaration that I am a sinner saved only by the grace of God."

"So, ignoring my little testimony and without acknowledging the possibility that he too might need some 'prison ministry,' the warden went on and asked, 'That was it? You were really hoping that Mr. Chora might produce a real article all about the "mighty man of God," and he was just hoping to spend more time outside of his cell?' And he went on to declare, 'You were using each other for your own personal gains.'

"That sounded so badly that I had to object. Yes, there was truth in there, as I had already admitted, but my original and continuing purpose was to be a witness to Chuck. I hoped that one or more of the people I told him about in such depth would ignite…something inside of him. I told the warden that I prayed to use the open door provided to me at the jail primarily to proclaim the mystery of Christ and to proclaim it clearly."

"Did he listen to that?"

"Well, you can bet that in the back of my mind, I was praying for him the whole time. I wanted to make the most of this opportunity, not only to get permission to meet Charles again in the privacy, so-called, of the conference room but to open a door into the warden's heart as well. And apparently, he did soften a little.

"I have learned that the main purpose of a warden is not simply to successfully 'contain' the inmate until their sentence is up. His true goal is to see each one benefit from their incarceration. To encourage growth and maturity and good fruit, like self-control, before they're released. Every warden wants for their residents what Jesus offers them. They can't say it, and they don't even need to use Christian lingo to describe it, but they all want to see their inmates impacted in a way that only true repentance can instigate."

"Okay, now you're just getting preachy. Did you do that to him too? And you're leaving out the one detail that would answer my question! Did he agree to let you continue the interview with Chuck as it was?"

"Yes! Yes, he did! Didn't I say that?"

"No! No, you didn't! Oh, brother, brother!"

"Well, he did! And so, I kept the arrangement Charles and I had for that next day to continue the interview. Tuesday the seventeenth at 1 p.m.

"I slept deeply in the front seat all the way there as Barn brought me over there again without Queenie coming this time, and Krispy pushed me in, much slower this time, and I will tell you all about it. But first, there's the meeting I had with Greg after the three of us returned to Chase Monday night."

"Slept in the car all the way…?" Macy asked, confused. "Meeting with Greg?"

"Yup. And you just won't believe it."

"Oh boy," Macy said quietly. "Can't wait."

CHAPTER 13

THE TOAST

"I was very glad I went to see the warden on Monday for several reasons. First, I succeeded in getting permission to continue meeting Chuck alone for the interview, so-called. Second, I got to share a little bit of my zeal for the gospel with the warden, Mr. Gagnon. And third, I found reason to relinquish my emotional connection with Queenie!"

"What? What in the world does that even mean?" Macy asked.

"Well, over four hours in a car with anyone tends to break down one's illusions about who they really are, don't you think? Well. Maybe not Barnabas', but my old, vague idea that Teddy was somewhat embodied in Queenie turned out to be unfair to all three of us, especially to Queenie. Of course, she has her very own personality, character, and temperament. Yes, Teddy impacted her for the good, but in a limited way. Queenie still developed along a personal route dictated by the full body of her innate character combined with her internally driven decisions. As far as what the future holds for her and Barn and Kris, they will be able to figure out which of them fit together if any of them ultimately do. I certainly don't have to worry about it.

"And there is one more thing that came of the long day away. We got home so late, after spending many hours in a fancy sit-down restaurant listening to Queenie critique the ambience, the menu, the food, the uniforms, and every move made by every worker on staff, that I got home very late and ended up meeting with *Greg* under some special circumstances!"

"So now you're telling me you had a *good* meeting with Greg?"

"Well, I didn't say it was bad, did I? Just unbelievable."

"Okay, well, please get on with the *unbelievably good* story already!"

"I didn't say it was so *good* either, did I? You know, Macy, I think maybe Chuck listened a little bit better than you do."

"I'll ignore that if you get on with the story," she said.

"Okay. It's a great story, and you're going to love it, in the end, I mean."

"Back in Chase," I quickly began before she strangled me, "we went to Queenie's place first to drop her off. And that took a while. They needed time alone to 'debrief' a little bit, I thought, after spending all day with me. I think I saw lipstick on Barn's face when he came back to the car. 'Isn't she great?' was about all he could say, several times, before we got to my house, and he helped me inside.

"A few minutes after Barnabas left, about 9:15 p.m., he called me to say that he thought he saw someone sitting in a car across the street from my house and that when the guy lit a cigarette, he thought he recognized Greg from church in the light. Barn just wanted to warn me that I might be called upon to do some late-night MG-type counseling, which happens once in a while. I hadn't told Barn about what Greg did to me on Saturday morning but told him 'thank you' and not to worry about it, that Greg wouldn't smoke, but thanks for letting me know, and good night, and see ya in the morning for another long day going to Riverside!

"I wasn't really too concerned at first. It probably wasn't Greg out there, and Greg *doesn't* smoke, I figured. But then, the more I thought about it, the more nervous I got. Maybe Greg *does* smoke, and maybe Greg *is* sitting outside waiting for the last of my lights, the one on my nightstand, to go out before he breaks in to attack me in my bed! I got myself worked up to the point where, finally, I had to go take a look.

"Shaking a little bit, I got myself back off the bed and back into my chair, wearing only my pajama pants. I had never realized before how much my floors squeaked as I rolled as quietly as possible out to the living room and up to one of the front windows. I felt pretty nervous and stupid. I was in my own house but sneaking around like a cat burglar. I held my breath as I pulled back the curtain a little to see if Greg's unmistakable fancy Lexus was truly and threateningly parked on my street.

"There it was! I would know that car anywhere. It was right where Barn said it was. I was able to peel back only the smallest portion of the curtain and kept watch for a few minutes to see if he got out with a crowbar or something bigger. But I was taken aback when a pickup drove by, and its lights shining into the car made it appear to be empty. That was concerning. He was already out of the car and probably sneaking around back where it was dark!"

"Where did that come from?" I asked Macy, as I suddenly noticed that she was writing notes in a spiral-bound steno pad!

"From my purse, where do you think?" she answered without looking up, and then asked, "So did he kill you?" and held a straight face while I thought about it.

"I thought you weren't going to write my stor—"

"I'm not! I might. We'll have to see if you ever finish telling it. Like, for example, what happened next already?"

"Well, I was thinking about how he accosted and assaulted me only two days before, so I started thinking about weapons! What weapons do I have in the house? Then I thought I heard a noise out back and started heading to the kitchen to make sure the back door was locked and maybe grab a knife. Stupid. What's a half-dressed cripple in a wheelchair going to do with a knife? 'Come over here and stand still, will ya, Greg? I'm gonna stab you in the knee!' I wasn't sure which was more pathetic: my inability to defend myself in a pinch or my complete lack of confidence in my God to help me.

"I pushed for the kitchen, but as I rolled by the front entry, the doorbell suddenly went off like a

EPAPHRAS: THE INTERVIEW

fire alarm! It spooked me so bad that I threw one wheel forward and crashed my bare left foot into the hallway wall! Of course, I couldn't feel it, but I knew I would have to check myself for more scrapes or cuts if I wasn't dead in a minute. Then I got mad, and all the fear in me disappeared! I turned back to unlock the door and confront the person I assumed was Greg! I wouldn't even need a weapon at that point.

"I started yelling 'Come in already!' before I even got to the latch but discovered that it wasn't even locked when the door abruptly swung open and stubbed all the toes on my right foot!

"Greg stumbled over me as he came inside, profusely apologizing for just about everything, and had to extract himself from me and my chair. When he was finally free, after stepping on all of my senseless toes at least a couple of times and steadily apologizing, he rushed straight over to my recliner in the dark living room and sat hunched down like someone trying to hide from, well, himself.

"Strangely, I realized that I was not at all surprised all this was happening! I almost felt negligent for not having the coffee ready and a snack prepared. Would *anything* surprise me this week?

"Anyway, I smelled cigarette smoke wafting out of

his clothes and figured he'd been sitting and smoking in the car for a long time. I still don't know if he was a steady but discreet smoker, or if this was an old habit reborn in stressful times, or some brand new affront to his heralded claims to physical purity. The question occurred to me, but I didn't really care about such trivia that night."

"Good! And I don't care about it right now. What happened next?"

"Yeah, yeah. I told Greg I was going to get some real clothes on, but before I left the room, I turned the overhead light on in the hallway and then quickly turned down the dimmer when Greg gave out with a little groan. It shed just enough light into the living room to show me that Greg had not only been smoking but sobbing for hours.

"I put a T-shirt on and a bathrobe but did not take the time to get it under myself, so it was just a knotty bunch behind my back all night. I was back in the living room in just a few minutes, but when I came in, I found that Greg had fallen back in the chair and was fast asleep.

"That was probably good for him, so I just waited and took advantage of the time to pray for him to find peace and for me to have wisdom and whatever else might be called for once we started talking. I had absolutely no idea what had been upsetting Greg these past few months. He had so long refused to become a real part of our group, to open himself up and share either interests or issues with the men, that he was now just a mysterious lone wolf and suffering for it. I sat and yawned and kept an eye on him and continued to pray.

"You know my life's motto, Mace: 'Wrestle in Prayer.'"

"Of course. You have it on the wall in your living room," she remembered. "I've been telling you to somehow include the Colossians 4:12 reference into the carving for years!"

"Right. Well, in that dim light, I could barely make out the words carved into that chunk of olive wood and hanging on the wall above Teddy's memorabilia shelf, but they were there and written on my heart as well. It was my truest connection to the biblical Epaphras, who Paul said was 'always wrestling in prayer for you, that you may stand firm in the will of God.' Very early on, this became key to my service to the Lord, and something that Teddy always encouraged in me.

"Then, as I looked around at the plaque and at

Teddy's memorabilia shelf in the dim light, I noticed that Teddy's bear, you know the one, was not in its place on the shelf! Ned made that shelf for me ten years ago, and the bear has not been out of its chair for more than a few minutes at a time ever since! I turned around and spun the dimmer switch all the way up and looked over at Greg as he stirred and squinted and swore in the bright light.

"Instantly and surprisingly, I felt enraged! He had actually taken my Teddy's bear off the shelf and held it with his stinky, tear-stained hands, and then he ended up falling asleep and let it get squished between his hip and the arm of my recliner where it might have been swallowed up under the seat cushion! I rolled at him like a Sherman tank saying, 'Give me that bear, you…' and snatched it away before it fell into the sinking abyss!

"Angrily and irrationally, I blurted out a dozen questions at once. "Greg!" I started, "What the heck is wrong with you? Why did you touch this? You smoke? What are you doing here, anyway? Why did you ask me about Teddy's killing and then come here in the middle of the night and take her bear?"

"I'm afraid I would have acted the same way, brother," Macy granted, and I just went on.

EPAPHRAS: THE INTERVIEW

"I placed my rescued hostage on my lap and backed as far away from Greg as I could get before sitting up straight as an arrow and glowering at him as if he had just sold me for thirty pieces of silver! But when it hit me that Jesus didn't even do that to *Judas*, I began to feel embarrassed and even ashamed of myself. A long slow sigh of hot air released my built-up haughtiness, and I sank back into my wheelchair in much the same way as Greg had shrunken into the recliner a little earlier. I noticed that I had tucked Teddy Bear into a tight spot next to my hip so he wouldn't fall under the armrest and under the wheels, almost in the same way that Greg had kept him safe by his leg.

"Then, in a flash, I realized that either I deserved the same degree of wrath that Greg had just received from me or that he might need and desire the same forgiveness and understanding I was freely and automatically giving myself. In this prayer match, I was pinned, and I knew it."

"Oh, Epaphras!" Macy gushed. "Such turmoil and such triumph!"

"Huh. I don't know about the triumph part. Sometimes I am so erratic. I want only to proclaim the mystery of Christ clearly! I hope you pray for me to that end, Macy.

"But yes, I was instantly convicted and instantly apologized to Greg for jumping on him like that. I went on to confess how I let my emotions lead me to judgment instead of letting the spirit of God guide me into forgiveness. And I promised Greg, and God, that I would strive to put the priorities of God's good and supernal kingdom first, instead of the inane and temperamental hazards of my own fiefdom."

"Were you being set up for something big, Epps? I still can't imagine what Greg was there to talk about, but it seems like you were being prepared to help him."

"You got it. And you will see."

"The situation was beginning to feel weird. Whenever I had encountered Greg in the past, he had always been the one talking. He was perfectly suited for his career in sales. He spoke loudly and clearly and was never at a loss for words. He had a thousand stories and could always pick one perfectly suited for the occasion and, without missing a beat, tell it with a mesmerizing charm and humor that would simply make one pull out his wallet and buy a matched set of whatever he was selling that day!

"But here he was in my house and hadn't said one

word since apologizing for that clumsy entrance, which was mostly my fault anyway. I decided I had to start drawing him out and get him on his way home soon. It was almost ten o'clock, and I had to go deal with *Charles Chora* again tomorrow!

"'Can I get you anything, Greg?' I finally asked. 'Would you like some coffee?'

"'That would be good, sir. But I don't deserve it. I really want another cigarette, but that's a bad idea.'

"I went and poured a big glass of cold water but had to ask him to come into the kitchen to get it. He did so and was so careful to stay out of the way of my chair as I made us some toast that it was almost awkward. He drank the water and then served himself another glass after asking if he could. And then poured another one to wash down the toast.

"'Why don't you deserve a cup of coffee, Greg? Let's talk,' I began when we were back in the living room with a couple of lamps turned on and without the overhead hall light blinding us.

"'Do you mind if I backtrack a way and tell some backstory? I think it will help.'

"Greg's backstory! I thought the day I heard something solid about Greg would be like the day they finally got to the bottom of the mystery of

Oak Island! But could something 'real' be found here? 'Yes, please' was all I could say, however, and he began.

CHAPTER 14

THE COFFEE

"Because I was aware of Greg's verbal prowess and his penchant for braggadocio, I deliberately set out to be wary of whatever he had to say. His smooth voice, combined with profound marketing and language skills, could be hazardous to the gullible and unprepared. I know I started out well because I remember thinking, 'Yeah right' once or twice, and then, 'Really?'; but I ended up finally with, '*Wow!* That's incredible!' Yes, I tried to resist falling under his spell, but it wasn't long before I became a true believer!

"In less than ten minutes, Macy, Greg convinced me that he had long been the victim! Repeatedly abused at home, cheated in school, defamed and maligned by friends, coworkers, bosses, and employers. He had been fooled by pretense and charm into marrying several women who turned out to be extreme reprobates. They all took advantage of his magnanimity and were miraculously able to convince the divorce court judges that *he* was the hurtful one. With the help of the corrupt judicial system, these women were able to confiscate all of his money and leave him destitute!

"Just about then, my eye fell on the curtain, still partially pulled back at the bottom, and I remembered Greg's shiny new Lexus parked outside. 'I can't even tell you of the horrid lies they told about me, Epaphras! You wouldn't believe it!' he was saying when the fog of lore dispersed, and I suddenly came around. I shook my head and said, 'Greg. What about *your* lies? Do you "deserve a cup of coffee" or not? I think you were at a strong point of weakness a little while ago. Which way are you going to go tonight? If you're not prepared to be honest with me right now, then go home and let me go to bed.'

"He looked stunned at my challenge, perhaps feeling the same way the naked emperor did when he was finally told outright something he already knew but hoped to cover up with a barrage of propaganda. I didn't understand why he would make such a scene at my house late into the night only to maintain the pretense of perfection for me. I suspected that he was actually ready to confess his inadequacies, but deep down inside, he knew it had to be all or nothing. He first tried the 'nothing.' Once that failed, he gave in to God and gave it the 'all.'

"'No, I don't deserve any coffee! Or anything else! I am such a liar and a fool and so arrogant!' And Greg broke into heavy sobs and fell forward off his chair onto his knees and elbows on the hardwood floor. I let him cry, and I prayed that God would shield him from embarrassment as he courageously unmasked and exposed the true truths of his innermost world to me, to himself, and to his Creator. I knew the Holy Spirit would lead him, in this state, to freely confess things that he long ago internalized but never realized had an impact, things that were underpinning the manifest sins people might point at without knowing the source.

"I sat across from him, praying for Greg and praising God for delivering him from the evil in his life. We suffer so from our own evil and from that of others perpetrated against us. Only God can sort it all out and place judgment where it rightfully belongs. Greg had opened himself up to God's cleansing, and God was hard at work doing just that in my little living room! I continued to thank God for His wonderful love for us.

"Greg stayed on the floor, bowed down before

his Savior and crying out. Most of Greg's prayers were muffled by his arms as he confessed his sins and surrendered, trusting himself into God's everlasting arms.

"I caught a bunch of words and phrases as he seemed to be rehearsing some pivotal times in his life. I heard 'daddy' and 'father' more than once. I heard 'fourth-grade teacher was right' and a bunch of other names. Perhaps some of the wives he wronged. If Greg was inclined to find and personally confess his guilt to all of those he thought of that night and to do what he could to make restitution, he would be very busy for a long time! This went on for quite a while.

"I heard 'Betty' and 'Todd' and 'Roberts' and—"

"Roberts?" Macy asked. "That's our last name. I'm sure Pete doesn't know Greg."

"Yes, of course. There are a million Roberts in the world. Who knows who Greg knows or knew back then.

"There were more names, places, and things, and even events, too, I think. He said something about 'love,' the 'fairgrounds,' 'matches,' 'gumbo,' and 'Massarotti' too. But, Macy, at one point near the end, I was pretty sure I heard Greg say 'Teddy' and then fall into terrible lurching sobs!"

"What? What about Teddy?! I'll kill him!"

"Oh no, sweetheart. It's not like that. Greg was inside Drakes when we were shot, remember? I had just walked past him on the way to the door. He did not kill Teddy!"

"Well, what then? I need to know what you know. Now!"

"I know you do. Just let me tell it all in order, and you will soon know everything I know and in the way it came out. Okay? Then you can write about it correctly too."

"I never said I wou—"

"I know. You never said you would. We'll see about that. But let me go on now.

"Eventually, Greg ran out of sins to confess. He went through his whole life, it seemed, with a fine-toothed comb and talked to God about every possible transgression he could have possibly made, including thoughts, words, and actions! Some of his admissions reminded me of mine, and I was right there with him at the foot of the cross, confessing and turning away from my own corrupt ways. When I opened my eyes, I became aware that we were both sitting in our chairs with our arms lifted up and praising God! We didn't talk about it or plan it, but we just ended up at the same place together! It was amazing!"

"Wow. God is so good!" Macy exclaimed.

"When I saw that, I just stopped in awe, and then Greg looked up and realized what was going on, and we both had a good joy-filled laugh. Again, I had to wonder what my neighbors must be thinking about the roller coaster of sounds coming from my house well after midnight!

"As we settled down to talk about God's goodness to us that night, Greg had one question."

"Something about Teddy?"

"Um, no, dear. He asked if he could have a cup of coffee! I laughed so hard at that! And I told him, 'You still don't deserve one, Greg, but by God's grace, you may have as much as you like!' and we laughed again while he pushed my chair into the kitchen."

CHAPTER 15

THE GUNSHOT

"I am fairly well exhausted," I said to Greg as I tried once again to get the knot of bathrobe arranged on my back a little more comfortably, "but I am dying to hear how this…whole thing… happened! Do you want to tell me about it? What's going on?"

Greg was almost giddy! I had never seen him like this before. "Yes!" he said. "I can tell you exactly what happened and when it started!"

"Great!" I said. "But first, let me recap what happened here tonight. Well, first, on Saturday morning, you came to MG early and got all up in my face and asked me about Teddy's killer and the police and stuff. That really freaked me out, by the way."

"I know it did! And I am so sorry for that, Epaphras! I didn't mean to do that to you. I was going mad with guilt and shame all week, and bothered by so much stuff, and…I don't know, but

I let it all out on you becau—for some reason. Will you forgive me?

"I know you're just the first person in a long list of people to whom I will be asking that question. God finally broke through to me tonight, and I feel his forgiveness! Thank you for not letting me get away with resisting him again!" Greg was ecstatic with relief and asked me again. "Will you? Forgive me, I mean."

"Yes, Greg, I know what you mean," I began. "And yes, I will forgive you. I am incredibly happy to forgive you! If only because I get great satisfaction in obeying my Lord, Jesus. Beyond that, I like trying to be like Him, and He is so forgiving of *my* sins. And also, because I love for others to know the joy and to live under the peace of being forgiven! And…there's always the selfish reason: because not forgiving you would only hurt me!"

"Well, that's a lot of good reasons, but I am fine with any one of them! I have been on the outside for so long, and I did it to myself."

"Well, tell me what happened this spring. Why did you start coming to church and to MG all of a sudden? And why did you barge in and hassle me on Saturday?"

"Well, I guess I have to say that God has been after me for a long time, but I always ignored Him or put Him off." Greg sat and looked at his feet. I thought he was about to cry. "It's funny that I always blamed God for allowing all the bad things that happen in the world to happen! You know? How could He let other people be bad and cause so much pain and trouble? But I never complained about exercising my own free will to do whatever sinful thing I wanted to do! If God had tied *my* hands or plugged *my* mouth, I would have resented Him for that too!

"It's amazing what just a little thinking can do for a guy. I had to admit that His giving us free will was the only way to go. Of course, His will is for us to live at peace with each other, but He has an even *higher will*! That we *freely choose* to live at peace with each other! What good is forced love? It's not.

"So, this spring, with these new thoughts swirling around in my head, I went to church as I usually did like once or twice per year to check 'Be Holy' off my list. But God saw me coming! Pastor what's his name was in the middle of going through Colossians, and I was there for the start of chapter three. 'Set your hearts on things above' caught my attention! I had always had my heart set on every other thing. Things 'below,' you might say. And he showed that there was a promise attached to the command. If I did actually set my 'heart' and my 'mind' too, it says, on things above, then 'When Christ appears…then you also will appear with Him in glory'!

"I wanted that, Epps! I wanted that bad! Or rather, badly!" and he looked at me and smiled at the joy of finding out about that promise! Old Greg, if he had made a grammatical mistake like that, would have made a big deal about it, to the point of making sure everyone who hadn't even noticed it was aware of the mistake, the excuse, the revision, and the etymology and use of the proper adverbial form of the word! I could see immediately that changes were already taking place in his life.

"But I struggled to make the decision. I saw that the next verse is the killer one; pardon the pun, please. It says, 'Put to death, whatever belongs to your earthly nature' and then offers a list of possible candidates deserving of the death penalty. You can look it up in Colossians 3:5 if you want to. I have been guilty of every item there. And then they're summed up to all be equivalent to 'idolatry'! Everyone knows how bad *that* is! I was buried in guilt!

"I don't mean to rehash all of those sermons that

the pastor already gave from that chapter, and I know you heard them all; you were there, but…wow, they struck home with me. Remember the warning attached to the instruction? I heard it loud and clear. 'Put these things to death because the wrath of God is coming!' I have been trying to 'rid myself' of the anger and malice, the filthy language, and the lying.

"But I just could not do it! Until now! Now, I have deliberately taken off the old self and have put on a new self that is already, I can feel it, being renewed in knowledge in the image of its Creator!

"And then the chapter goes to the most beautiful promises! I can't wait to walk freely with God's chosen people and to be 'dressed' appropriately in compassion and patience and the other 'clothes' mentioned there that I forgot."

"Macy, I was blown away to hear Greg talk like that! And to see that he had pretty much memorized those verses in Colossians too, and especially because he must have done that even before he really accepted the truths found there, or at least before he had given himself over to it as he had just done in my little living room. It was amazing and humbling!"

"You got two of the five items of spiritual apparel Paul mentions there in Colossians 3:12, Greg. He says, 'Clothe yourselves with compassion, kindness, humility, gentleness, and patience,'" I said, filling in the qualities Greg missed and admittedly trying to show off a verse or two I had memorized. "And he goes on to say, so beautifully indeed, 'Bear with each other and forgive whatever grievances you may have against one another. Forgive as the Lord forgave you.'

"Yes, I forgive you, Greg, and ask that you will forgive me for judging you so harshly and for so long. I put you in a box. But our Lord has rescued you."

"Greg just looked at me for half a minute before exclaiming, 'I put *myself* in that box! And I locked it from the inside! I would not ever think to blame you or anyone else at all!' And he watched me go limp with relief and sorrow. 'If it helps, Epaphras, I certainly do forgive you, "as the Lord has forgiven me!"'

"You really did memorize that whole chapter, didn't you?" I said, laughing and choking up a little.

"Chapter?" he said, "I memorized the whole of Colossians a month ago! And His Word has not returned void! Woo-hoo! And *that* is from Isaiah 55:11!"

"No, it never does!" I said and acknowledged,

THE GUNSHOT

clothing myself in a small "T-shirt of humility," that I wasn't sure where that verse was from before Greg said so.

"Now, Greg," I said and looked at the clock as it was ringing out 2 a.m. "Are you okay to talk just a little more? I have a feeling that while you probably came to me because I lead the men's group and I am available to help the guys when I can, there's more to it this time."

He looked at the floor, thinking. But his head shot up when I went on with, "Does it have anything to do with me in particular, or...Teddy?"

"Wha? Where did you get...? Teddy? Why would you...?" I had never seen him unable to speak clearly and coherently before that very moment, and I felt sorry for Greg and scared too, but pressed in.

"Well, on Saturday morning, you leaned into me with questions about Teddy. And earlier tonight, or maybe I should say yesterday evening when you were confessing and crying out to God, I was pretty sure I heard you say her name!" And he turned beet red!

"Please tell me, Greg! What was it? Why....? Did you....?" And it was my turn to be all flustered. "I need to know...whatever...it is."

He choked and stammered a little, and cleared

his throat, and looked at every object in the room including my chair, my feet, my ear, but not my eyes. I let him take his time, but it was killing me! I could not imagine!

"Well," he started, slowly and quietly, in a strange voice seemingly dampened by penitence, "you know I was at Drakes that night, right?"

"Yes, Greg. I know," I said in a way I hoped would be rushing him to *quickly* relieve me of my need to know what he thought he had to do with Teddy's shooting!

"It was before we ever met. I was so into my own thoughts and disturbed by my poor marriage that I barely noticed you two at all until I glanced over and saw your beautiful wife, Teddy, sitting quietly and looking down at the table while you stared at her. I had no idea what she was thinking, but I could surely feel that there was something good going on between you two. Am I right?"

"Yes. Go on."

"I am sorry, Epps, but it was something I did not recognize and could only interpret sexually. You caught me looking at her, and I wanted to act like I was someone who understood the mystery as if my wife and I were on the same super plane of intimacy, so I winked at you, trying to be a part of your vaunted club, as it were."

"I didn't say anything but marveled at his description of those very memorable events. His memory exactly matched, and perfectly contradicted, my own!" I told Macy.

"Then she suddenly jumped up," Greg continued, "and walked out! I am more used to *that* happening, to be sure, but I knew she wasn't *walking out* on you; she was inviting you to follow! Who knew a couple could be so in tune with each other?

"As you both headed toward the door, my now first ex-wife and I looked at each other, both of us frustrated with things the way they were but so totally unable to understand. We had nothing like what you had. More like the exact opposite, in fact. I wanted to be *rid* of my wife, and you were chasing yours down, having been invited to take her home."

"Well… so what, Greg?" I sputtered out. "What does all of this have to do with…anything?"

"Then I heard the gunshot and thought, 'Victor!'"

CHAPTER 16

THE PROFILE

"Who in the world is Victor?" Macy wanted to know right now, and she jumped to her feet!

It was times like that that I really missed my working legs! What a strong statement one can make simply by standing up! All of a sudden, I felt so jealous!

"Hold on, will you?" I said, "Sit down!" daring to stifle her zeal with my envy. "I had the same question, but it took a while to figure it out. I wondered if it could be the same Victor who was in my high school class. The one Zoe had lived with for all of three weeks before she somehow got *him* kicked out of the apartment *he* had rented from *his* father for them to share. The one who had struggled and struggled with life until he found the Lord and is now a thriving member of the MG!

"But Greg never really met his Victor and never heard his last name! I asked him, 'Who is Victor?

And what did he have to do with the gunshot?' I was all over him, Macy, practically forgetting that we had just bonded in the spirit and were moving forward with forgiveness and unity and brotherhood and blah, blah, blah! I was dismayed at how fast and furiously I became unglued! Poor Greg!"

"Poor Greg *Schmeg*!" Macy cried and stomped one foot, causing me to covet her abilities again. "Why did he suspect some unknown 'Victor' of having something to do with killing my sister-in-law if he never met him or whatever? That's crazy!"

"I know, I know. Let me go on already, will you? I know how you feel. Please sit down now, honey, and catch your breath, okay?" She glared at me but then listened to me. I watched with astonishment as she slowly sat back down and deliberately slowed down her breathing, closed her eyes—though some tears were seen trying to squeeze their way out under quivering eyelids—spread her hands out in front of her with palms down, and stretched her shoulders upward until the back of her neck disappeared.

After a minute, she regained complete control of herself and said, "I'm okay now, Epaphras. Thank you. Please jump ahead or something and tell me… did Victor shoot our Teddy?"

"No. He did not." And then, risking my own life, I said, "I don't think so."

"What?" and it seemed when she jumped out of her seat for the second time that she was about to pounce on me, wheelchair or no wheelchair!

"No! I am sure I know that he did not!" I finally declared. Macy sat back down with a thud. "Anything is possible in this world, right, Macy? But if you want my opinion, it couldn't have been Victor."

Macy burst into tears which quickly led to horrible sobbing. She did not want "my opinion." She wanted facts. It had been so long!

I knew she loved Teddy as a sister and that they had become extremely close. I knew that as a new police officer at the time of the shooting, in line to one day become a detective, Macy wanted answers! Even though she worked in another state, she had gotten herself deeply involved in the early investigation at the small-time Chase police department.

Macy and her husband, Peter, flew in immediately after the shooting, of course. Or so I was told when I awoke after having been unconscious for several days. They were not yet there during the emergency surgery when the doctor located the bullet stuck in my spine and found and repaired the damage done to my intestines made along its path. At first, when he found the bullet, the surgeon only suspected that I might be paralyzed, but he did warn the family it was possible. Macy was in the room later when I came to. She waited stoically and optimistically but was devastated when I began to realize I could not move my feet or legs.

Poor Macy. She was shattered. First, because her sister-in-law, who was also her college roommate and best friend, had been shot and killed, and on top of that, her brother was shot and found to be paraplegic!

Macy went on to be dumbfounded and outraged that the "local yokels" were unable to find a single clue after the shooting and did not have even one lead to pursue! She made a pest of herself at the police station and embarrassed the department with complaints and insults before getting her emotions out of the way and settling down. But then, with a clear head and a professional approach—her natural good looks and charm contributing—Macy did end up ingratiating herself with the force.

In the end, she confidently told me that the Chase PD had done everything they could and that she approved the final report. I counted on that assessment to get me through the long, frustrating years of inaction that followed.

Nobody knew anything about the shooter. Not the why or how, and certainly not the who. The police were as frustrated as Macy was for the lack of any kind of a lead. No witnesses. No surveillance footage to collect from along the street back in those days. No forensic evidence could be found at the scene. Nothing was stolen or missing. There weren't any disgruntled anybodies we could think of. The only people who might have seen the shooter at all were me and Teddy that night. And I surely could not see anyone in front of Teddy.

Nobody knows if Teddy saw her killer, let alone if she would have recognized him…or her. I only saw Teddy silhouetted in a muzzle flash for a split second before I heard the bang and before the blow of her weight was thrown against me, and I went down halfway back into the doorway at Drakes. I know I didn't see any form or shape of a person who, the police say, must have been only ten feet away from Teddy.

I know that while, at first, I was so anxious to find out who did this to us, I eventually became entirely obsessed with the "*why*" question. "*Why* would someone want to shoot Teddy? Teddy, of all people!" My real interest in discovering the "who" was only to understand the "why."

As Macy calmed down, again, and lifted her head, I saw that she was a mess. Thankfully, there was a box of tissues at hand. I first gave Macy a big wad, but when that proved insufficient, I handed over the box and waited while she caught up with herself.

"Let me tell you what I do know, Mace," I said quietly. She blew her nose one more time and nodded.

"Do you remember that I told you before that Greg said he was hoping to 'rid' himself of his wife?" Macy nodded silently and looked stricken. "Did he really mean…?"

"No, he didn't. But he hated being married to her or to anyone for that matter. Greg had really wanted to get married but had all the wrong reasons. He was really just thinking about advancing his career and attaching himself to her family fortune. At the same time, she thought she was getting a great prize, but quickly found out Greg was really just a great schmoozer. He had her fooled into thinking he was a truly thoughtful and kind man who would cherish her and treat her like a queen. The self-deceiving ruse was mutual, though, and so was the disappointment and the heartbreak."

"I know that happens, Epps. You know Peter and I had issues to work through, and it was hard, even with God's help, but...what did Greg do about it?"

"Not much, really, but of course, nothing good. Mainly he was just stupid. Feeling sorry for himself, he went to Stan's place for a sub on the Friday before the shooting, and it was like midafternoon, a very slow time of day there. Stan was out for supplies or something, so his girlfriend, Joanna, was working, and she was the only one there, and so after making his sandwich, she sat down by him."

"Uh-oh."

"You know this song?"

"I've heard the tune."

"It's got a bad melody," I said, and we shook our heads at the cliché-ridden speech we both learned from our dad. "Anyway, as Joanna fawned over him, Greg quickly got around to griping about his wife. They were married on the twelfth, just like Teddy and me, but on a Sunday in 1998, so they were at Drakes for their first anniversary that Monday night. By the way, so were Oscar and Hannah and Yeti and Ralphie! All of us were married on July 12 in different years. But like good people everywhere, most of *us* were wed on a good ol' Saturday!" I said, poking the bear, just a little.

"Please go on. But maybe it's time for you to forgive Peter and me for having a *Friday* wedding during the second month of your first-year teaching, and you had to get a substitute teacher, and he was an idiot, and your class fell behind, and you got a bad review, and it was all our fault. Even though Teddy also took the same day off, and her class thrived under her highly professional care. But please, go on."

"Uuh, yeah, so… Okay. I forgive you," I said rather graciously. There was never any shame in being bested by Teddy, or Macy, in anything.

"So, Greg was not looking forward to Drakes," I went on, while Macy, in the likeness of Charles, made some large letter notes on her pad and underlined them emphatically. "Greg's wife was making him go out to Drakes so they could at least pretend they had a good marriage. Greg was telling Joanna all this—so way out of line—when a scraggly looking character that Greg never saw before came in and said, 'Hiiiiii, Joaaaaana. Yer lookin' *good* for an old lady!' She was twenty-nine to his twenty-four! Greg stood up quickly and glared at the guy as if he would be Joanna's knight in shining armor and protect her honor, which seemed to scare the guy pretty good. Joanna shushed him back into his seat and stepped behind the spit shield saying, 'Hi, Victor. I thought Stan told you not to come in here anymore.' Greg jumped up again and said, 'Is that right? He's not supposed to even be *in* here?' Victor anxiously backed toward the door looking from Greg to Joanna and back again, and said, 'But Stan's not here, is he? I saw him leave before to make sure. I'm *hungry*, Jo!'

"Rather than fight with him, Joanna gave Greg a reassuring look and hurriedly made Victor the cheapest sandwich they sold, his usual, collected his payment in change, and told him to sit by the front window so he could watch out for Stan and 'run like crazy' if he saw him coming. 'I will!' Victor assured Joanna. Then she sat down by Greg again.

"But then, with an audience in the room, instead of complaining and blaming her for everything, Greg started boasting about his oh-so-beautiful wife and how much he cherished her and how he didn't know what he would do without her.

"He even described their plans for Monday night and what they were going to wear and how much he

EPAPHRAS: THE INTERVIEW

expected to spend for the best steaks Drakes has on their opulent menu, etc., etc."

"Oh no!" Macy exclaimed. "Your friend Victor was after Greg, or maybe…what's her name, Greg's wife to get back at Greg! And he…instead…"

"But no, he wasn't! And no, he didn't!" I virtually shouted at Macy before she had the chance to fall apart. "Victor would never have hurt a fly, let alone some strange woman he had never met! And he wouldn't ever think to threaten someone like Greg for pushing back at him. He was so extremely… reticent, so shy, about everything. Even the bullies in school left him alone because he seemed to think he deserved the bad treatment they tried to give him, and it was just no fun."

"But why did Greg think…? I guess it just made sense to him that it might have been Victor."

"Maybe," I said, "but Joanna didn't help. While Greg was going on, trying to build his own stupid ego with all the boasting in front of Victor, Joanna thought it would be fun to goad Victor a little. She called to him across the room, saying, 'Hey Victor, would you be willing to go to Drakes Monday night and make sure no one hurts Greg's wife? Greg will give you twenty bucks, I bet!'

"'Who me?' Victor objected. 'I could never hurt anyone in my life. I never did.' And just then, he saw a red truck coming up the street and got scared. 'Stan's coming!' he said and ran to the door, knocking his empty sandwich wrapper and bits of tuna and toppings on the floor. Then he thought better of using the front door and ran into the darkened back room. Joanna and Greg both heard a big crash and an 'Oooof!' and thought he ran into a stack of boxes of supplies. Then there was a scramble of feet and frantic searching for the back door.

"Greg was watching the front door, getting himself ready to deal with Stan. 'He's not coming back today!' Joanna said, noticing Greg's anxious glances at the front door. 'You're a piece of work, aren't you?' she said.

"Joanna laughed at Victor, telling Greg that Stan was not expected back for hours and that if he did show up, he would park in the *back*, besides!

"'What a loser!' Greg said, laughing at Victor's clumsy flight, and he finally heard the back door close with a bump.

"Then Joanna laughed at Greg, too, for all of his false bravado, the platonic infidelity she was so happy to take advantage of, and his obviously insecure pride, and when the time was right, she would be happy to tell Stan that *all* the men in Chase were losers.

"Joanna took care of the garbage on the floor, wadding it up and tossing it out while she continued laughing out loud at poor Victor."

Macy wasn't laughing at all. "Are you sure," she said, "that Victor had nothing more to do with it, Epps? I understand that he doesn't really fit the profile, but I want this settled so badly!"

"I understand, sweetheart. You know I do. And I want the same," I said, reaching over to hold her hand. "But there's more to this story."

"Oh no! And yes, please," she said, conflicted. "I can't take much more of this, but what is it, Epaphras? Tell me already!"

CHAPTER 17

THE GARBAGE

I went on to tell Macy, "I called Victor right away; I mean Monday night, while Greg was still at my house! Sometime around 3 a.m., I think, I called Victor and woke him up! He and his lovely new bride too! They've only been married since around last Christmas, you know.

"Victor now sleeps the sleep of the redeemed and so deeply that he never hears his phone. His wife answered his phone pretty much in a panic, thinking the worst, of course, as people do when the phone rings late at night. I had to apologize to her about ten times and try to explain again and again that I simply had a couple of questions for Victor that were very important to me just then. When she finally admitted that she could trust me with Victor even at this hour, she went to work to wake him up for me and handed the phone over to him.

"'Good morning, sir! What can I do for you?'

EPAPHRAS: THE INTERVIEW

Victor, too, was perplexed by the call, and I had to repeat a short version of my explanation for calling at this hour, but he was able to allow for odd behaviors in odd folk like me, and said, 'No problem.'

"Before I tell you about the call, Macy, can I offer one important insight into Victor? Something he told me a few months after he was saved and delivered from an empty, miserable life without Christ."

"How can I say no to that?" she said, "But please make it quick!"

"I will, Sis. You see, I never knew Victor back in those days, and so I scarcely believed it when he told me this part of his story: He said that ever since he learned to write, and for many years after, he whispered to himself, 'Yeah, right!' every single time he wrote his first name!

"I started to cry when he told me about the miserable set of lies and the burden of foolishness that he had been told and believed and carried for years. I hate what people do to each other, especially what parents do to the children God puts in their care. But while I was tearing up, he started to chuckle and then suddenly burst out laughing! Then I caught on and started laughing too! Irony of ironies, Victor had become a *real* victor! An overcomer in Christ! And that's the Victor I have known and loved ever since!"

"Wow. I wanted to kill him a few minutes ago. Now I want to give him a hug!"

"I know, right? And now whenever I hear his name or even think of him, I think of Jesus, the ultimate Victor, and my faith is seriously boosted every time!"

"Okay, but back to the call already!" Macy said with a big smile.

"Okay! Well, Mace, I didn't hold back. I dove right in, 'Victor, did you have anything to do with Teddy's shooting?'

"He dropped the phone! I heard his wife say, all muffled, 'What happened?' and I think Victor asked her to turn the other light on. 'I dropped the…can't see it. It must've…anded upside…' And then I think he stepped on it. 'I found it, honey, thanks.' His voice sounded more agitated than a dropped phone would cause, and I began to worry about how he might answer my question.

"'Sorry, Epps. I dropped the phone. Somebody… beautiful…got lotion all over it,' and I could hear the smile in his voice as he teased his bride. I gasped in relief and laughed out loud!

"'You asked about the shooting? If I had anything to do with it? Wow! No, I did not! Where did this come from? And at…in the middle of the night, may I ask? Are you okay?'

"'Yes, I'm okay,' I said. 'I've been talking with Greg. You know Greg, right?' I answered.

"'Sure do. And especially since he's been back at church regularly lately and coming to MG meetings, too, for a while now. Why, Epps? What's going on?'

"'Did you know Greg back in the day? He says he ran into you just a few days before the shooting. And,' I hesitated to say the rest, "that when it happened, he suspected *you*, or at least somebody named Victor, right away!'

Victor involuntarily tried to sit down on the edge of the bed but missed and slid down to the floor, bumping his tailbone on the bedframe. He was too stunned by Greg's claim to feel the pain.

"'He was at Drakes that night. Can you remember why he might have thought of you? I just want to verify, or rather, check, his story from another perspective.'

"'Oh wow!' And I heard Victor's wife say, 'What? What? What's going on, Victor? Are you okay?' Then Victor tried to cover the microphone, but I heard him say, '…my…bone….be all right…you everything after, okay?...it's Epaphras....trust him always...'

"That muffled endorsement made my day, by the way!

"When he came back on, I could tell he was in a different room and getting comfortable for a long talk. 'Wow, Epps, isn't that like ten years ago? Did I even know Greg then? I don't know what he's talking about.'

"'Thirteen years and four, er, almost five, days ago now. I didn't know Greg then either, but he had a wonderful encounter with God just this night, Victor; in fact, he is still here with me at my house now, and we're trying to figure something out,' I elaborated as best as I could, but I was trying not to instigate any false memories.

"Greg was paying close attention to the conversation on speaker, and when he heard me mention his 'encounter' with God, he stirred a little and smiled. Then he looked up, and I saw him mouth a 'thank you' to God.

"'I see. Praise God! I am so happy for Greg! God is so good to us!' Victor took the time to exclaim and to share with Greg in the joy of his redemption. Victor always makes me smile! 'Can you give me any clues on what I'm supposed to remember? What day of the week did we meet, if we did? And where?'

"'Well, I was trying to not lead the witness here, as it were,' I said, and Victor added, 'What *year* are we talking about? Can you tell me that much?'

"'It was 1999, and so you were like twenty-four years old. In the summer, and it was July…9, a Friday.… afternoon,' I said, hoping I didn't give out too much.

"'1999,' Victor repeated. 'Ah yes, one of my glory years,' he said through a very audible smirk. I could say the same thing about those years, but without the sarcasm. My life with Teddy put me at the top of all heaps! We were deliriously happy together, and nothing could go wrong. Until it did. 'They always say to "hold on loosely," don't they?' I asked myself.

"And Victor continued. 'I was…not doing much of anything in those days, Epps. I couldn't get away from living at home. I had no work ethic and such low confidence I couldn't keep a job very long. My dad said I still owed him for his raising me, so when I did have a job, he made me sign all my checks right over to him. I was selling my plasma for spending money then, too, but I never did anything bad, Epps. You know, like criminal.' And he paused for a moment to praise God. 'Wow! God has brought me so far since those days!' and then he paused again to wrack his brain. 'Let's see. Friday afternoon, July 9, eh? I got nothing. Any more clues for me?'

"I looked over at Greg who was sitting with his elbows on his knees and his head hanging down. He was desperate to have his story corroborated but truly afraid he would find out that I was all wrong about Victor and that maybe he *did* shoot Teddy and me and all on account of his own stupid pride. But if Victor did do it, he was sure doing a great job of playing dumb!

"I was way too tired to have this game go on much longer, so maybe I got a little careless with my probing.

"'You went in somewhere for lunch that afternoon, Victor. What did you like to eat? Better yet, what place did you specifically like to go into to eat but were kind of afraid of the owner?' I offered, thinking that I just gave it all away, and either he would now just guess the place I had in mind and leave me with doubts, or I would find out Greg was still just a lying liar lying like a rug. I did not want to have to deal with that!"

Macy was on the edge of her seat even while I was just telling her the story!

"'I used to like to go into Stan's sub shop when I

could collect enough change for the Tuna Buna, as I used to call it. But Stan didn't like me, so I didn't go there much.'

"'Bingo!' I said exultantly and with great relief. 'That's it! That's where Greg saw you that day! Now, do you remember Joanna? She eventually left Stan and went back to her family upstate, I understand, but she worked in the shop at times that year.'

"'Oh yes. I didn't know she had another family somewhere. That's weird. I remember thinking she was very pretty at the time, but that might have just been me. I see everything different now. She was good to me, though. Why?' Victor asked me.

"'Well, she was there the day you met Greg in the shop. And some…other stuff happened. Do you remember? That Friday afternoon? Had Stan told you not to go in there for some reason?' I asked him.

"'Oh yeah! *That* day! *That* was Greg? I never made the connection before now! The guy who was looking for a fight or something. He scared me, so I just ate and left. Yeah, and now I remember that I ran through the back room in the dark and ran right into Crash and a bunch of boxes!'

"'Wait! You crashed into a bunch of boxes?' I was confused.

"'Yeah, and Crash too,' he said. 'Knocked the wind out of both of us but I managed to get up first and got out the back door and took off.'

"'Wait! Victor! What do you mean "the both of us"? Who else had the wind knocked out of them?'

"'Crash! Oh, now I see why you're confused. I ran into this guy back there. A guy called Crash! He was in the back room, and I cras—ran right into him! I never did find out what he was doing back there. Or if Joanna even knew he was there. Knowing him, he snuck in and was looking for stuff to steal.'

"Greg's head had popped up! Then he stood up, and I probably saw exactly what Victor saw and was afraid of that day! Greg could, as I had learned a couple of days earlier, be very imposing when he was motivated! And then, at the same time and in the same melodramatic cadence, we both said, '*Who is Crash?*' as if we had practiced it for an hour, so Victor got the question in stereophonic splendor!

"'Um…hi Greg,' Victor said sheepishly. 'Am I on speaker? That's okay. Um. Crash was just some guy used to live somewhere in Chase, I guess, and was always up to no good. He was always looking for someone to join up with him in petty crime and general mayhem.'

"'That's it? Is that all you know about him? When was the last time you saw or heard of him being around here, Victor? Do you know his last name?' Greg had taken the phone from me and was holding it close to his mouth and shouting into it even though the speakerphone was on.

"I signed for him to give it back and to sit down, which he did, and then he started pounding one fist into his other palm. I was a little taken by the fact that he was more zealous to solve this mystery than I was.

"Victor was answering the questions Greg asked as I tuned back in: '…was the last time I ever saw him. Last time I wanted to, too. I bet he was mad that I knocked him down and maybe got him discovered in the back of the sub shop. I saw him kind of hobble outside and shut the door when I was down the alley, so I don't think Joanna found out. Did she, Greg?' Greg shook his head at me, and I told Victor he said no.

"'His last name, you say? I don't even know his first name. I don't think his name was really Crash.'

"'Ask him if Crash knew him. Was he maybe looking for Victor Monday night?' Greg pleaded. 'Cause if he heard all of my stupid bragging garbage and then heard Joanna telling Victor to go there…'

"'Crash didn't know me. Nobody knew me,' Victor said painfully, having heard Greg's question. 'And it was so dark in there anyway; I only recognized him when he came out into the light just before I went around the corner. He had kind of a big head.'

"'Don't we all,' Greg muttered."

CHAPTER 18

THE JOKE

By the time we got through talking with Victor, I was exhausted; Greg was exhausted; I imagine Victor and his wife were exhausted too. Macy was exhausted from hearing about the drama I had been going through and from reliving so many difficult emotions, and we were all distraught from discovering so much information that had been so well hidden for so long!

In just a few days, I had gone from the simple but potentially worthwhile effort of getting my testimonial story sorted out and recorded for the sake of advancing the kingdom of God to struggling with the conniving Charles, reopening the wounds of my grief, suspecting Greg's complicity in murder, discovering a connection between Teddy's death and my friend Victor, and then learning about some unknown reprobate named Crash who may very well be my Teddy's real killer!

But what could be done just then? The sky was lightening in the east when Greg, wiped out but elated at the same time, finally left for home. I rolled wearily to my room and "crashed" myself! I was wonderfully relieved to get away from the sweat-soaked bathrobe balled up on my back all night and to stretch out on my bed, where I passed out in a moment!

Next thing I knew, Barnabas was knocking on the doorjamb to my bedroom, and seemed to be in a state of shock, having found me "sleeping in," as he called it. I barely had time to get ready for the long drive back to Riverside, but with his help, I got cleaned up and dressed and even ate a bagel before we hit the road.

Barn was so taken with my story as I shouted parts of it across the house from one room or another in the rush that he didn't even get to mention any of Queenie's latest charming phrases or mannerisms until we got to the car. Thankfully, at about the same time, I leaned my head against the door and fell fast asleep before we were even a block away from my house! Later, and in no time at all, as he helped me wake up and get into my chair outside the prison, Barn told me that he spent the drive praying for me for peace and for a good resolution guided by God.

THE JOKE

Such a good friend! And aptly named, as Barnabas means "son of encouragement"!

I felt odd going into the jail that day. In one sense, it felt like I was doing something normal, continuing the series of planned interviews that were all arranged with Charles, but on the other hand, things were different now. I was aware that Charles could not possibly write a good article, let alone a book, that he had summarily tricked and used me, and I was unaware of whether the warden had let him know the jig was up.

There would certainly be an interesting dynamic today, anyway. Chuck wouldn't be able to just ask me about his note. He would have to pretend everything was normal. Any revelation of a change in circumstances would be in my hands and at my discretion. And I wasn't at all sure how to proceed. I was still so tired and in turmoil about this "Crash" character! Could he really be the culprit? And could he ever be found now, so many years later?

The guard had "placed" me inside the conference room and left me alone while he went to get Charles. It was almost one o'clock, and I thought, somewhat crankily, "*I* was up all night and had to drive over 130 miles, but *I* made it on time!" as if I hadn't slept, drooling on my shirt, all the way there while Barn did the driving. "Am I even prepared to be ministering to prisoners, let alone one that I'm kind of ticked off to, or with, or at, or whatever I'm supposed to say?" I decided to sit still and pray for this meeting. I could not manage it well without God's help; I knew that much.

About ten after one, a stern-looking guard I had never seen before returned with Charles in tow and, after checking it over again for contraband, handed Chuck his bag of devices and notebooks. Chuck came in, all excited and talking fast. "I didn't really expect you today, Epps, for some reason," he said, glancing at the guard as he stepped outside and closed the door. Then he looked blatantly up at the camera and told "me" how he must have forgotten all about our meeting, and that was why he didn't even have his equipment packed up to come down here when the guard came for him! "Crazy, huh?"

Once all that was settled, Chuck got busy setting up his recorder and unpacking notebooks and a couple of pens. He found that the battery was dead but plugged his charger into the wall and hit "record."

I was not so excited. Nor feeling any personal warmth toward Chuck. Just love. "It's been a looong weekend, Charles, since we met last," I began. "Do you remember what we were talking about at the end of the day on Friday?"

"Yes, I do. We talked a lot about Oscar and then nothing about Hannah. I wanted to hear the great love story, but you were too stubborn and wouldn't tell me."

"Something like that," I said, annoyed at the attitude. "Do you remember that what I really wanted to tell you was the great love story about you and God? About how much God loves you and gave Himself up for you so that your sins could be forgiven."

I stopped there to get his reaction. It was unhurried in coming. He slowly deflated—shoulders, spine, arms—and slumped against the wall behind him. His eyes glazed over, and he seemed to look around the room for something not-me to stare at. When his eyes fell on the recorder, he reached out and turned it off with a dramatic flick of the wrist. With confidence in the Lord and in the power of prayer, I said, "Today of all days, I think you will want that on," and I stared him down until he almost sneakily restarted the recorder without taking his eyes off of mine, and only then broke eye contact.

EPAPHRAS: THE INTERVIEW

"What is up with you today, Mr. Mallas? Are you okay? You seem very tired. Are you sure you want to be here?" and he began to turn against me and my agenda.

"Absolutely, Chuck! I am all in for you and here for your good." And I reminded him that he suggested to me on Friday that the only reason we couldn't get into the gospel message then was that he had "already knocked on the door," too bad, so sad. I could tell that he remembered perfectly.

I had his attention. And leaned into it.

"Do you like spending time with me, doing this research, Charles? This is an awfully big project you've taken on. Are you sure you want to keep coming down here? This could take months, possibly, and maybe you won't like being away from your regular room so much." His eyes flickered at me momentarily when I called his cold gray cell a "room."

Without waiting for an answer, I added, "Anyway, I think that if you are going to be describing my work with the MG with any understanding, you will have to at least have an intellectual understanding of my faith. Don't you agree?"

"Hmmm," he granted.

Genuinely curious, I asked, "What do you know

about the Christian faith and worldview, Chuck? Did you have any exposure growing up? I don't know anything about your early years, or how you ended up getting in trouble with the law, or anything else for that matter. Did your family take you to church?"

"I am not here to be interviewed by you, sir. You've got it backward. I am only here to find out… about you and your work, with the Emgee thing, or whatever you call it."

"'Men's group.' The letters *M* and *G* stand for men's group," I tardily explained, apparently remiss. "It's just one of the ways my church serves its members and the community at large. Healthy men make for a healthy family, which makes for a healthy neighborhood. What was your father like? Did he have any help? Was he there to teach you about being a man?"

"My father was fine. My mom told me that before he left, he kissed me on both cheeks twice."

"Where did he go?"

"Oh. My mom never told me that part, but my sister's dad went to the army, so he probably did the same thing. He knew how to be a man, and so do I. It's easy. What about your dad? Did he love you and cuddle you and teach you how to build stupid birdhouses or something? Who needs that?"

"I'm sorry, Charles, but you needed that. Still do. Maybe not the birdhouses, but you need to know how to build a life. And you need some solid building materials. God can provide, and does provide, both the instructions and the resources if we ask Him to."

"Why would I ask 'Him' for anything? I'm doing fine right where I'm at," he said, and just then, I heard the distant sound of a metal door clanging shut. If Charles heard it too, he ignored it brilliantly. "I'll be out of here soon, and I'll get a job at a magazine or a newspaper or something 'cause I'm really good at words."

"You stink at words," I declared unapologetically. "At least the written word." It was time for truth. "But more importantly, you are a sinner, just like everyone else in the whole world, and you need to confess it," I said, not knowing what kind of reaction to expect. He didn't even flinch. "Remember how Teddy forgave me so quickly when I was trying to blame her for making us late to Drakes? She was ready to. And God is always ready to forgive you for anything; for every sin you've ever committed!"

Before I mentioned Teddy, it seemed like Chuck

was working up to an eruption, but then he wound back down and started to listen instead!

"He can't, though, until you confess that you're a sinner. Do you admit that you have ever sinned at all? It only takes one sin to make a sinner," I pressed in. "One lie makes a liar."

Charles nodded slightly. "Of course," he said.

And in an effort to console him a little, I told him that the Bible says that *all* have sinned! Everyone that was ever born! "Not everyone is man enough to admit it, though, like you just did."

"So, then what?" Chuck asked, dismayed. "Do we all go to jail or get sent to you know where? I mean, what's the point?"

"Good question! And the answer is '*No*'! God says that we all *deserve* death because of our sin, but Jesus, God's Son, came to earth to bring us the *gift* of eternal life in God's presence! God showed His love for you, Chuck, by sending His Son to die for you even before you confessed your need! It's all good news!" Chuck was too stunned to even smile, but I did see his eyes begin to water a little as he looked at me, receiving.

"Maybe you feel like you need to do something for God to earn such a gift, Charles, but you don't! You don't have to 'put in your time' or 'finish out a long sentence' or anything but receive the gift. Most people want to serve this great God after they've discovered His goodness and mercy to them, but that's a response of gratitude and not paying for something as if anyone could ever afford such a treasure."

"I never knew! This is too much!" he said, amazed.

"There's more!" I told Charles, and he looked at me warily. Perhaps he thought I was about to disappoint him by showing him some fine print about tithing or good works or with a list of sacrifices he would be required to make. "Not to worry, Chuck! All you need to do is tell God that you agree with Him about the situation."

"I don't know any prayers, though. What do I do?" he asked so sincerely.

"It's not like that. Prayer is just talking to God, and it doesn't even have to be out loud. You just need to confess—" I began, but he interrupted me.

"Confess what? Everyone knows what I did. It's in my record already."

"Nothing like that stuff, sir. Here, let me write down two verses that summarize what I mean. Then you can read them and make sure they make sense to you. If you agree, then just turn the ideas there into your own prayer, either out loud or silently in your own heart.

"Okay?" I asked, and when he agreed, I asked him if I could use one of his notebooks. He handed over the larger one, and I opened it to find a blank page. I saw a lot of scribbled notes and a bunch of stick-figure drawings. At a glance, most of those looked tragic and fearful. There were several good drawings of pistols being fired, with large flames coming out of the barrel and bullets flying. One full-page drawing showed a stick figure with a large head hanging from some very solid-looking gallows. Gruesome pictures that I hurried past to find an open sheet while praising God for delivering my new brother from his sin!

"I memorized this one just for an occasion like this, Charles, and I am so happy to share it with you! This is from Romans 10:9–10, and it goes like this," and I began to write it out as neatly as possible.

"If you confess with your mouth Jesus as Lord, and believe in your heart that God raised Him from the dead, you will be saved; for with the heart a person believes, resulting in righteousness, and with the mouth he confesses, resulting in salvation."

Charles read it over slowly once and then read

it again twice. "That's it?" he asked incredulously. "Speak it and believe it? And be forgiven? I can get 'rightessness' and salvation in a minute and without money or sacraments or a priest?"

"That's what it says, Charles," I said, as I started to feel the warmth of God's love for him welling back up in me. "That word is 'righteousness,' and it means morally good. We admit that we are sinful—*not* righteous, and then if we believe in the risen Lord Jesus, He *makes us* righteous! And millions of people have found it to be true and life-changing. God's love is so great, and His mercy and grace are so…amazing! That's why we gather at churches to learn more about Him, to share the joy with other believers, and to give Him thanks and praise. We don't have to do anything to *earn* His salvation, so we spend our energies praising Him and serving His purposes."

"Talk about getting off easy," I heard Chuck more or less mumble, and I took it as his first prayer.

"Would you like to pray through that verse now, Charles?" I asked, and he reacted like a little boy who was told he should go ask a cute girl to dance. I understood that feeling. I remembered feeling rather intimidated when I got up off the floor and stood in that hallway with Teddy looking at me with her beautiful, kind, green eyes and that sweet smile! My knees were knocking, and I burst into a cold sweat! But not because I had made a fool of myself in getting her attention; it was because I found that she favored me with her attention despite my foolishness! All of a sudden, today, Charles received an invitation to walk into the throne room of God Almighty! Of course, he was in some form of sublime shock!

"I do. But would you help me?" he asked shyly.

"Absolutely!" I said. "How about if I run through what I think you should say based on those verses? I can even write it down if you want."

"Yeah, let's do that, but no need to write it down. I'm pretty good with words… not writing them, but saying them," he said, smiling at me.

I felt honored by his humility. "It would just go something like this, and you can change whatever you want to, of course. 'Dear Jesus, I do confess, or admit out loud, that You are the Lord. I want You to be the leader of my life instead of me. I do believe, Lord, that God raised You from the dead. Please save me from my sins.'"

"That's it?" repeating what he said earlier. "It

seems so simple, but I can tell that says it all. It's just so surprising and wonderful that God doesn't make it all complicated and hard for us!"

And then Charles bowed his head and folded his hands like a pro and pretty much repeated the prayer as I had said it. And with so much sincerity and sweetness that my heart completely melted right there in that cold, stark prison room. I cried tears of joy and humility, feeling incredibly grateful that God would use me to help this man repent of his sins and come home to God.

Neither one of us even thought about the camera and the microphone surveilling us. We felt very aware, however, of God's Spirit there in the room, comforting and loving us both.

Chuck never did knock on the door; he didn't want to stop the conversation we were having on such a wide range of subjects, and neither did I! He opened up freely about his upbringing and the hard time his mother had while raising him and his half-sister by herself. He always missed having a dad around like some of his friends had even though they complained about their dads all the time!

Chuck even started telling me about the crimes he committed that put him here in prison. Starting with the most recent when he tried to push a lady off of the edge of a scenic overlook. The judge didn't care that she jumped out of the way just in time, and he fell and slid off the edge onto a rock shelf eight feet below and broke an ankle. He said he always pretended to be mad at that judge, but he knew all along that he deserved the full sentence even as if the lady had been killed. I could see why he said he got off easy!

Before that, he pushed a lady in front of a train! Fortunately for her, he didn't time it very well, and she just got up and stepped off the tracks in plenty of time. There were enough witnesses, one of whom was the train engineer, but Charles got off with only being convicted of a Class C misdemeanor battery, which put him in jail for half a year back in 2005.

I was beginning to think he was trying to get caught when the guard came along and ended our session. For the first time, *he* knocked on the door before coming into the room. Charles greeted him with a smile and a bright "Hi, Guard Fitzgerald! I am forgiven! Praise God!"

I watched as they went around the door and into the hall. Guard Fitzgerald said, "Good. It's almost time for chow. Maybe they'll ask you to say grace."

EPAPHRAS: THE INTERVIEW

Chuck leaned back and laughed as if he had just heard the best joke in the history of jokes. As he tipped backward, hooting, behind the window in the closing door, he smiled broadly at me, and I noticed an optical illusion in the glass and thought, "My goodness, but he has a big head!"

CHAPTER 19

THE RIDDLE

Barn and I returned to Chase in plenty of time that Tuesday evening for me to meet up with Peter and Macy, who had just come to town that day to stay at Peter's family home through the coming weekend. The three of us had dinner, and then Macy and I went over to my house to talk. I told her everything that was going on, all of the details up to and including the point of Charles' wonderful conversion! She had told me that she would consider taking over for Charles and writing the story about Teddy and me and the whole MG ministry.

At the very end of the evening, the question of Crash was bothersome, of course, and still lingering, but we both felt a very real comfort in having even one possible lead in the case after all these years. Macy planned to go down to the Chase PD in the morning and see what they knew about an old delinquent from way back named Crash.

EPAPHRAS: THE INTERVIEW

The next day was Wednesday. I called Macy late in the morning as soon as I could and told her, "Get to my house! *Now!*" I was somewhat surprised but very grateful that all she said was, "Okay." I did not want to explain my adamancy over the phone.

I wasn't treating her fairly by being so abrupt, but I was just passing on the treatment I had received earlier that morning when I took a call from the prison warden at 5:42 a.m.! "Get over here *now!*" he had said once he was sure I knew who it was on the phone.

I told him I would and began to get ready to go, but first, I passed the warden's odious treatment of me on to Barnabas. I called him immediately and said, "Get over here *now!*" but added, because I am not as gruff as a prison warden must be, "Back to Riverside we go!" Amazingly, he was at my door and looking not at all rumpled in only twelve minutes! And that was after stopping to fill up the car and grabbing us a set of four large, assorted gas station muffins!

Good thing I was up around 5 a.m. and already about half ready for the day when the call came in. After yesterday's exciting ministry to Charles and being a witness to the way God brought him to salvation, and enjoying a regular praise service with Barnabas in the car all the way home, and even after spending so much time with Macy, I was in bed at a decent hour and slept like a rock. I woke up early and continued rejoicing and giving thanks to God for what He had done for Charles!

As I washed up and started getting dressed for the day—a day *without* expecting to endure that long drive to Riverside—I fell into seriously praying for Charles on his first day as a new believer. There's nothing necessarily easy about being born again! It's the most wonderful thing a person can do, but it can also be heart-wrenchingly painful to go through at the same time. There are so many challenges to face, so many confessions to make. Sometimes friends and family don't understand what's going on and may be worried, or worse, imagine ways to take offense. There are so many sudden realizations to be had as the eyes are opened, as if for the first time, to truth.

Even while a person may feel totally new and like everything is different, so many things and people are still tragically the same, and that can be unsettling. Charles might be a "new man" inside, but he would still be waking up in prison just as he had for over five years already and would be going through the same routine as any other standard, security-driven, typical prison-protocol day of the continually incarcerated. He would need regular prayer coverage, and I planned to ask all the guys to keep him in prayer at the next MG meeting a week from Saturday, if not before.

When the warden called, and after I had a chance to get over my first impulse toward anxiety, I figured that poor Charles was already dealing with some of these "new believer syndrome" effects. I would be glad to sit down with him and help him through it. I was a little bewildered by the warden's seeming panic, but this was my first experience with witnessing to a prisoner, and the situation was bound to come with some unexpected complications.

Barn and I had a fine early morning drive to the east. It was unusual for the visors to come down and be put to use when we were driving *to* Riverside, but they worked just as well for the sunrise as they did for the sunset. I was left hungry by my generosity after I let Barn eat a third muffin, which rightly should have been my second, but it had somehow been polluted with coconut topping, so it was no big loss.

I even nodded off for a half hour or so and then woke up fresh and ready to help Chuck adjust to his new life in Christ. I prayed for God's wisdom and reminded Barn to keep us all in his prayers today, and I also asked him to pray for the warden. He needs the Lord too. Barnabas assured me he was already praying along all of those lines.

When we drove into the parking lot, I saw a bunch of people standing outside the visitor entrance area, and they seemed to be waiting for us! I saw the warden looking around anxiously before he recognized us pulling off the frontage road. Then I noticed Krispy and another guard or two that I had seen before, but there were another half a dozen guards standing neatly behind the warden. "Must be something they do on Wednesdays," I thought.

A woman was walking back toward the building, and the warden turned to yell something to her. She looked over her shoulder and then picked up her pace, almost running back toward the building where a guard stood, ready to release the door and let her inside.

"Good morning, Warden Gagnon," I said as we pulled up and I rolled down the window. "This is unusual. What's all the fuss about? Is Mr. Chora okay?"

"Good morning. Oh, Mr. Chora is fine. Big changes. Big change in him!" And then, to Krispy, he said, "Get him out of there, will you?"

Kris jumped into action. Barn too. He popped the trunk open so Kris could get the chair out and then came around and helped me get prepped for the shift. Kris was unfamiliar with unfolding the chair, so Barn stepped back to help him. In the slight interim, I thought I saw a familiar car turn in and maneuver quickly into the maze of employee vehicles opposite us. Kris must have asked a dumb question about the leg supports or something because I heard Barn murmuring, "They're here." A minute later, Barn was moving the car, and Kris was rolling me toward the entry with an entourage of about five people, and I felt silly. And worried. "What in the world is going on?" I asked myself, but more so of the Lord, because I knew that He did, in fact, already know the answer, whereas I did not have a clue.

There was a traffic jam at the doorway, so we came to a stop, and I could catch my breath. Kris was, of course, at his professional best, working especially hard to impress the warden while he had the chance to work in his presence. But while we were stopped and waiting, he slid one hand off the wheelchair handle and patted the top of my shoulder. I greeted his friendly gesture with a smile and patted his hand, making sure, first, that the warden was looking the other way. I am so blessed to have such good brothers! And I thanked God for putting Kris here right when he did!

Once we got inside, my "entourage" split up and headed off in different directions. I expected to be taken down the usual route toward the monitored conference room Chuck and I had been using, but the warden led Kris and me toward his office. There was no usual search of my person, no emptying pockets, and no interrogation regarding the "purpose of my visit." I had to sign no papers releasing liability in case I was kidnapped or murdered or tricked into thinking I would soon be made rich and famous for my biography.

All kidding aside, I was dumbfounded.

Charles was sitting in an armchair in front of the warden's desk, and another guard was standing behind him with his hands on the front of his belt. Even though I could tell he was an experienced prison guard, he looked a little confused at this proceeding, although he was obviously attentive and ready for anything.

I could tell by four small indents in the carpet that another chair had been removed to make room for my wheelchair. Numbly, I looked around for the missing chair and found one matching Charles' placed off to the side of the desk but not against the wall. Curious. With a hundred unknowns to consider, with Charles' poor heart in turmoil, I wondered about an errant chair.

Mr. Gagnon directed Kris where I should be parked, facing Charles more than toward his own seat, where he went around to and sat down heavily. He looked very tired, like he was here all night, or at least, very early. I was surprised when the warden then said to the other guard, "Jeff, you can go now, but please wait in the outer office." After he stepped quietly out, the warden said, "Kris, why don't you sit here?" pointing to the odd chair, which was now a little behind and to the right of me, answering my little concern and also raising my tension, all at the same time. "Why would he invite such a new guard to remain in a counseling session, let alone to sit down?

Finally, I put my petty questions aside and focused on my new brother in Christ, Chuck. He looked awful! Like he hadn't even slept. And judging by the ink stain I remembered seeing the day before at the bottom of the pocket on his orange jumpsuit, he hadn't even changed clothes since yesterday. And I tried to remember if I had noticed a difference in the jumpsuits between last Thursday and Friday. "How often do they change them?" I wondered stupidly and almost asked out loud.

Instead, thankfully, I looked again at Chuck's very sad countenance, comparing it to the huge joy-filled smile he had at the end of yesterday's meeting when I saw him through the window as he was leaving the conference room. Strangely though, something about that image kind of bothered me now.

"You are a new man in Christ Jesus," I said to Charles. And I suddenly remembered something that Greg was talking about, "When was that?" I asked myself. "Just Monday night or more like Tuesday morning. Maybe only thirty hours ago!"

"There is a passage in a letter the apostle Paul wrote to the Colossians, in the first few verses of chapter 3, that says, 'For you died, and your life is now hidden with Christ in God. When Christ, who is your life, appears, then you also will appear with him in glory.' All is new, Chuck, and all is forgiven, and you are tucked away safely in the arms of Jesus, and Jesus is securely held by the Father!"

Charles broke down, plunging forward in tears, arms hanging toward the floor, head bobbing with each deep sob, and almost falling out of his chair! I tried, with all I had, to jump up and catch him, but I couldn't, but Kris could and did and was gentle with him and held him until he pushed himself back in his seat and could at least continue crying without the danger of hitting the floor. I never felt so helpless and useless as I did just then. I not only wanted to catch him but couldn't; I wanted to comfort him but did not know where to begin because I did not know what was wrong.

As soon as Chuck was stabilized in his chair, Kris turned away and went back to his seat. On the way, I noticed him give the warden a glance that spoke of frustration and impatience.

Incredibly, Mr. Gagnon followed up on the hint! He said, "Okay, Cr—Mr. Chora. I think it's time for you to tell Mr. Mallas what's on your mind today."

Chuck looked horrified and, sobbing, said, "I ca… I can…t."

"Yes, you can. And you must, and you will," the warden said with all of his official authority. "You told your cellmate; you told a guard; you told me around midnight. It's time."

And God's sweet spirit came over me. I felt wrapped up and held in His arms. Jesus was with me so closely, and I never felt more "in" Him than I felt just then. I could finally admit to myself that I knew that Charles was Crash and that Charles had killed my Teddy and paralyzed me.

I did not know why, or how, or anything else about that night. But I knew why I was brought here this morning. The warden thought I was here to hear Charles' confession. But I was here to give my forgiveness, in Jesus' name.

"It's okay, warden," I began without looking at him. "He'll say it when he's ready to."

"But you don't understand…" the warden started.

"Yes, I do." And then to Chuck, I offered, "What I told you yesterday. It's all so real, my friend," and Chuck burst into more sobs but glanced at me fearfully until he recognized the truth of God's love on my face.

Kris was suddenly standing behind me with a hand on my shoulder again. I looked up to see him staring at me as if a Christian is not *really* expected to act like Christ. Later, I would have the chance to assure Kris that God was empowering me at that moment and that we can *really* expect Him to do that every day!

"Did you shoot Teddy, Charles?" I asked gently.

"Yes, I did. I…did," Charles confessed in deep

EPAPHRAS: THE INTERVIEW

sorrow. "No excuses. I am so so so very sorry, but it was me, and I did it."

"Charles," I said solidly and waited for his attention. "I do forgive you."

The warden interrupted the pivotal moment to say, "You did what, Charles Chora?" And only then did I notice the small camera up in the corner of his office. Chuck looked at him and then up at the camera.

"I, Charles Chora, confess that on the night of July 12, 1999, I was messing around with a gun I stole from the sub shop outside of Drakes restaurant in Chase. I thought I might scare a guy that I said beat me up, but he really didn't. He just ran into me. And he wasn't even there. Then I thought I might rob some rich guy and his wife who was a jerk. Not his wife, the guy. I was by the curb pretending to be a cowboy or something, and the door popped open, and I turned, and my arm swung up, and the gun just went off, and I ran away."

"Did you shoot the gun?" the warden asked.

"Yes, I guess…I mean, I did shoot the gun."

"At the people?"

"Not on purpose. Not on purpose, but the bullet did hit the people. Two people."

"What do you know about the people in the doorway?" the warden asked.

"It was a couple," Chuck answered. "A very beautiful woman with a name called Teddy, and her husband who is Epaphras Mallas, which means bricklayer."

The warden looked at me. I looked at him. I think he was expecting me to get violent or to at least show some anger, and he was ready to call the other guard in, perhaps thinking Kris would beat on Charles for me if I asked him to and imagining that the other guard could stop him.

Then he turned back to Chuck. "What happened to the two people you shot, Mr. Chora?"

Up to this point, after his original breakdown, Charles was able to describe the events rather matter-of-factly, but with the last question, he started to get emotional again. "Oh, God! I am so sorry! I don't deserve anything good from You! Your mercy is amazing, I know it!" and he paused before being silently prompted by Mr. Gagnon again. "I know, judge, I mean warden; When I shot the gun, I killed the woman, Teddy, who was so good of a person, and I paralyzed the man, who is like her a lot too."

I was not watching Chuck. Just staring at the

floor but listening to every word. I noted that he was ready to admit to every degree of culpability; he was not trying to shirk any of it. And I noticed, too, and smiled to myself when he, after learning so much about Teddy and me in the past week, said that I was like her! It was the very nicest thing anyone had ever said about me! And the fact that I could appreciate it in that moment told me that I had truly forgiven this man who had taken from me as much as anyone could without having taken my very own life.

After waiting a moment, "Is there anything else you would like to say, Charles?" the warden offered.

I looked up and saw that Chuck was about to spurn the offer, but I caught his eye, and he said, "Yes, thank you, Mr. Gagnon," and he took a few seconds to collect his thoughts.

"Thirteen years and six days ago, I did a terrible, terrible thing and seemed to get away with it. I got away with murder. I guess some people do. But only from the law. Inside, I was driven to get punished, to pay a penalty. I started doing things to other women but made sure they did not get hurt too bad. I made sure I got caught, and I always pleaded guilty because I always was guilty, and I mean since even before shooting…Mrs. Mallas, Teddy."

At his mention of her name, I finally broke down and wept heavily. "My Teddy!" I cried. Chuck paused; the warden waited; Kris got up and walked all the way around behind the warden to grab a box of tissue he spotted there. He came around the front then and gave me the box after pulling a few out for himself.

I felt no embarrassment, no rush, no compunction to make it brief, but cried it all out. I was discovering how grief-stricken I truly was down deep, and then I discovered a refreshing well of relief flooding up and over my soul. For the first time since that fateful night, I felt at peace!

And at the same time, I felt a desire to reach into the lives of others I knew who could use a drink from that well. Even in that chair, with the tears flowing, I was praying for Zoe and Hannah and Ned and Stan and Ralphie and Wade and Updike, asking God to use me if He could to bless all of them.

After trying and failing to blow my nose discreetly, I came up smiling and said, "Please go on, Charles. I am sorry to have interrupted you." Mr. Gagnon looked at me and blinked, and signaled for me to pass him the tissue box. He wiped his face and waved impatiently at Chuck to go on.

"I was just saying that I am guilty. But starting yesterday afternoon, I am also forgiven! And I am thanking Jesus for forgiving me and making me 'rightness' in Him," Chuck said, without having mastered the Christian lingo quite yet!

"Me too!" I said rejoicingly.

"Me too!" Kris agreed, but more quietly.

"Myself as well, I am sure," said the warden, if only not to be left out of the pool.

"I praise God for His forgiveness," Charles went on, "but I know that the state does not do that so much. I will not fight whatever sentence is given me by a judge and maybe spend many years in jail with the warden."

The room exploded with laughter! Kris lost all of his professional cool, I did a quick 360 in my chair, guffawing all the way, and even Warden Gagnon started cackling so much that he tipped back in his chair until it crashed into the credenza behind him, and we all laughed and pointed at that too! Jeff, the guard waiting in the outer office, unexpectedly burst into the room with his hand reaching for the sidearm he used to carry before becoming a prison guard, ready to quell a riot! We were all stunned into silence for a second, but then with Charles joining in, all four of us burst out laughing at the look on poor Jeff's face!

The warden was still laughing while he motioned for Jeff to relax and to close the door. Jeff closed it, this time remaining inside, and that made us all laugh yet again. Jeff stood there speechless and stared and wondered while the rest of us caught our breath and tried to recover.

After what seemed like an hour, the warden finally addressed Charles, "Charles, may I call you Charles since we are going to be spending so much time together in jail, right?"

Charles, who only after the fact realized the joke, said, "Why, heck, you might as well call me Chuck!"

"Fine," the warden said, and having decided that he had now laughed enough for this month, added, "Thank you for your comments. I should think that with your obvious repentance and mature attitude, your guilty plea, your willingness to take full responsibility for your actions as a troubled youth, and with Mr. Mallas' support and, er…statement of forgiveness before him, your sentencing judge is likely to be quite lenient."

"Thank you for that, Warden, but whatever my state sentence is, I am committing the rest of my life to the service of others and making sure they know they can be forgiven of anything by Jesus."

The warden sat for a second, taking that in, and then said, "That is highly commendable, Charles. I mean, Mr. Chora." Then standing up and leaning over his desk, "Jeff, will you give these men a minute to say goodbye and then deliver Mr. Chora back to his cell?" he said while scribbling and palming a short note.

"And Kris, I will ask you to do the one more chore we talked about for Mr. Mallas, and then please spend the rest of your shift in the Public Relations department across the hall," he said while slyly handing me the note on his way out of the office. Kris smiled and nodded and said, "Yes, sir! It will be my pleasure, Mr. Gagnon!"

"The PR department across the hall?" Jeff was saying to Kris as Kris nudged him out of the room and shut the door, leaving me and Charles alone.

"I think you made quite an impression with Mr. Gagnon, Epps. I hope you can talk to him some day like you talked to me about the Lord," Charles said.

"Me too, Chuck. Me too," and I waved the note at him. "He turned the camera off in here," I said.

"Wow!" Chuck was amazed. "I think that's

probably not legal. Maybe he will be in jail with me after all!" And we laughed out loud again, as only brothers can.

We only had a few minutes, and we used them for crying a little and praying for each other. I always love the simple, heartfelt prayers of a new believer like nothing else!

At the end, Charles wanted to ask me a riddle he had made up just the night before. "Really, Chuck? Okay," I said. "Let's have it."

Charles said, "What did God say to the devil, again?"

I thought I knew what the answer might be, but I let him play it out. "Hmmm," I said, and then, "You tell me, Chuck. What *did* God say to the devil, *again*?"

"Checkmate!" he said. "Checkmate!"

EPILOGUE

This time, *I* got to "knock on the door," and when I did, Jeff came right in to walk Chuck out. We bade each other a short-term goodbye, as I would certainly be back to visit soon, although not necessarily as soon as the Thursday visit previously scheduled; I had a lot to process! I threw one more parting promise to Chuck as he left: "The MG will be praying for you fervently!"

Then Kris came back in, looking like a cat with a toy mouse, and grabbed my chair. "What happy potion did *you* swallow?" I asked him, but he just smiled even more broadly and pushed me out, fairly skipping behind me! I was intensely curious to find out what he was up to and also shaking as the morning's revelations started hitting home. But when he stopped and went around me to open the door to the hall, I said, "Wait! I need to give Macy a call! She was going to the police station in Chase this morning to find out about Crash, but now I can tell her I know who he is and where he is!"

"You can do that later, Epps! She can wait." Kris told me uncaringly. I was shocked and dismayed at his callous attitude! "Kris! How would you feel? I'm surprised at you!" He was looking frustrated with me but found and pushed a doorstop in place while I pulled my phone out and dialed. "This will only take a minute. And I don't care about your stupid prison PR team anyway. That's just stupid!" I added so eloquently.

The phone rang once, and Macy answered. I barely heard her as she seemed to be whispering. "What is it?" she said. I whispered back until I realized that was silly, "Hi... Are you okay? Hey, get to my house *now*!" All she said was, "Okay," but there was a weird echo, and I added, "I'll be there in a couple of hours." I ended the call but still heard another echo of her saying, "Okay!"

Without any signal from me telling him that I was ready to go, Kris suddenly pushed me out through the doorway, and, unbelievably, there was Macy just coming up the hall! She dropped her phone into her purse and laughed delightedly! Then she ran the last few steps toward me, with tears starting, and threw her arms around my neck! "It's all over!" she said. "It's all over!" I answered joyfully!

Kris, the compassionate, said, "Not quite. The warden wants Epaphras to meet the team down the hall. I have my orders, and they are waiting for us now." I was about to throw a fit, but Macy touched my arm and, looking at Kris, said, "Oh. Okay. Whatever you say, Officer. Right, Epaphras?" I swallowed my frustration and accepted my duty with a good old "Yes, dear." It's always a good idea to appease one's sister, so off we went again, perfectly in line with the orders Kris was given. I had to admit that since the warden was so very good to me and to Charles this morning, obliging him for a few minutes was probably worthwhile.

But I didn't even have time to ask Macy what in the world she was doing there! "The police must have identified Crash for her and told her he was presently confined at Riverside as Charles Chora," I guessed. Then to relieve Macy of any fears she might be having that we would next be facing a long, tedious trial, I craned my neck around and called over my shoulder to Macy, walking behind us, "He confessed! He confessed the whole thing!"

"I know! I know! Isn't it great?" she said.

Only a few yards down, there was a double door with a sign reading "Conference Room," and we stopped in front of it. "Macy, what do you mean, 'you know'? Kris, can't this wait? Do I really have to meet the PR team right now? I don't want to…" Kris sighed and pushed the door open.

There was no Prison Public Relations team inside. Instead, the room was nearly filled with members of my own men's group team! Yeti and Ralphie and X-Ray were there, and Victor, and Barnabas, and even Greg, and even Macy, along with Kris, were there at the prison to greet me and to strengthen me and to encourage me and, truth be told, to carry me through the shock of the great mystery being finally solved. At the sight of the love and concern on so many warm faces, I broke down and cried, both in the joy of the Lord and in suddenly missing my Teddy more than ever.

Very early that morning, Warden Gagnon had called Kris into work and told him about Charles' confession. Kris went right to work on the phone and, with permission, informed and invited this wonderful group of friends to come and be ready to support me.

I was quickly mobbed and smothered in hugs and kisses and handshakes and pats on the shoulder! It was a wonderful, last-minute gathering of prayer partners, and I loved every minute of it!

I heard Kris, several times, telling somebody, "He forgave him! He *forgave* him! I saw it myself!" Once everyone was caught up on the recent events, I had the team gather around, and we gave God thanks and praise for all He had done, especially for saving both Greg and Charles in the past couple of days! Jesus' work on the cross bought forgiveness for them most recently, but the rest of us all remembered that by His grace, Jesus had done the same thing for each of us. Then we prayed together, particularly for Charles, for me, and for Macy, for the long-term future impact of the MG, and finally, some of us may have asked God to say hi to Teddy for us and to tell her we love her.

PLAYER	BORN	MARRIED	THE INTERVIEW 1999/2012	THE APPOINTMENT 1990/94/98	THE ENGAGEMENT 2006	THE OPPORTUNITY 2016
ARTY	1957				M	m
BARNABAS	1985		M		m	M
CHARLES	1982		M		m	M
DRAKE	1952	1985	m			M
EPAPHRAS	1974	1997	M	M	M	M
FRANCINE	1983	2016		m	M	
GREG	1974	'98, '04, '16	M		m	M
HANNAH	1952	1975	m	M		m
ISAAC	1977	2011	m	m	M	M
JOANNA	1970		m	m	M	
KRISPY	1983	2016	M		m	m
LENNY	1973	1998	m	m	M	m
MACY	1976	1997	M	M	m	m
NED	1980	2016		m	M	
OSCAR	1950	1975	m	M		
PETER	1973	1997		M		m
QUEENIE	1989	2016	M		m	M
RALPHIE	1968	1986	m	M		m
STAN	1966			m	M	m
TEDDY	1975	1997	M	M	m	m
UPDIKE	1960	1985	m		m	M
VICTOR	1975		M	m	M	m
WADE	1945	1966	m	M	M	
X-RAY	1978		m	M	m	M
YETI	1968	1986	M	M	m	m
ZOE	1975	2016	M	m	M	M

M = Major role
m = minor role

APPENDIX:

CHARACTERS PLAYING MAJOR AND MINOR ROLES IN COMING SEQUELS

The chart found to the left includes a list of my twenty-six "A-Z" characters that live in or about the town of Chase. You will recognize many of them from *The Interview*. Some will return to play a role in one or more of the forthcoming sequels (or prequels, as the case may be) along with other characters not yet introduced. The chart also shows the year or years in which each book is set, important dates regarding births and marriages, and a layout of which players will play a major or minor role in each book.

ABOUT THE AUTHOR

It's no surprise that Mike Miller's writing has now extended into the wonderful world of fiction, and Christian fiction readers will be delighted with this author's artful pen strokes, finding friends (and troublemakers?) amongst the interesting characters developed within the pages.

Everyone's lives veer off their planned course, and Mike's journey has not been immune to life's redirection at times, but he has always kept the compass aligned with his spiritual north, Jesus Christ.

Despite life's ups and downs, Mike has managed to keep his heart fresh, open, and young.

A widowed father of three grown children, Mike has recently remarried and relocated across the country, where his new bride, their overzealous grown "puppy," and their involvement with ESL training and videography at church keep their life together both rich and busy. Their hearts are full with eight grown children and seven grandchildren.

Printed in the USA
CPSIA information can be obtained
at www.ICGtesting.com
LVHW011840300823
756768LV00007B/76